In Spite of *Ourselves*

(A Murphy Brothers Story)

The Potter's House Books (Two)

BY
JENNIFER RODEWALD

Jennifer Rodewald

"*But the greatest of these is love.*"
1 Corinthians 13:13

Chapter One
(in which Jackson faces his disaster)

Of all the ways he could have imagined this weekend going, this had never entered his mind. Not once. And if someone had told him it would happen this way, he would have laughed in their face, said *Not in a million years*, and gone on his way.

Jackson Murphy wasn't that kind of man. Hadn't ever been.

Hiding in the luxury hotel bathroom—with the door locked—he lowered his towel-wrapped, exhausted, and hungover body to the edge of the massive soaking tub as glittery speckles of steam drifted around him. That helped the surreal, this-can't-be-happening sense that made his already throbbing head spin.

He glanced at the phone he'd left on the pristine marble counter while he'd showered, now afraid to pick it up again. Needing to pick it up again. Terrified to see what he couldn't believe play out on the screen yet one more time. Compelled to watch, hoping that this time what had been there before wouldn't be anymore.

It'd all be a lie. A prank. A massively disturbing dream. He was, after all, the master prankster.

Swallowing—man, it was hard to breathe! And, did a hangover come with the shakes? He'd not had many, so he wasn't sure. Admittedly, a few, but not enough to decipher normal hangover instability from extreme. From his hands to his chest, he trembled violently. Not to mention breathing about as smoothly as he had round about mile twenty-two the day before.

Maybe someone had slipped something into one of his drinks?

No. He knew that hadn't happened. He had enough memory intact to know he'd done this to himself.

Had he really done this?

The compulsive demand to see it for himself—*one more time!*—had him reaching for his phone.

Connor's text was still open.

What the—Jackson! Are you kidding me with this? Dude, what are you doing? This had better be one of your jokes, man.

Above that text, there was a video attachment. From Jackson. Of Jackson...and the woman who was on the other side of that bathroom door.

Mackenzie.

Mackenzie-he-wasn't-positive-of-her-last-name. Except, now he was pretty sure that whatever that name had been before last night, now it was legally Murphy.

He didn't want to, but he tapped that video, and the screen told him what only fragments of his memory could recall. There they were, Mackenzie and him, in one of those tacky, drive-through, do-something-stupid chapels. Doing something incredibly stupid.

Completely hammered Jackson Murphy took totally drunk Mackenzie Thornton (that had been her last name!) to be his lawfully wedded wife...

The video cut and then picked up after the blessed ceremony, capturing the newly wedded pair in front of the door to the room he'd woken up in. With her in his bed.

"Hey, you two!" Some stranger—who sounded a bit slurred himself—called from outside the shot. "Here's to doing something crazy!"

Drunk Jackson and inebriated Mackenzie threw their arms up and cheered. For their idiotic selves.

"Just married!" they cried.

Watching, Jackson's stomach lurched. Again.

On screen, drunk Jackson lifted his loopy *wife!* and popped open the door. That was why he knew it was to this very room—

in the background, the scene glimpsed the king-size bed that was beyond the bathroom, where he was currently hiding. Their honeymoon suite. That should be a nice, enormous charge on his credit card.

Not to mention the rock he'd glimpsed on Mackenzie's hand before he'd made a sneaky getaway to the bathroom. Had that thing been real? Good grief. He was an electrician, with a few side gigs as a stand-up comedian. He lived on cheap fast food and frozen boxed dinners, making rent paycheck to paycheck, and he certainly hadn't been saving any funds for a diamond.

"Here's to happily ever after, you crazy kids! Enjoy the honeymoon." That voice was a woman's. Also one he didn't know.

The video stopped. He assumed the person who had recorded it handed him his phone. He could also assume that he'd sent that video to his brother before the honeymoon commenced, because Connor had sent a string of texts that lasted from 1:00 to 6:00 a.m. None of which Jackson had seen until the morning, because he'd apparently shut his phone off.

Or hit Do Not Disturb. Like every other groom in America would. Nausea rolled hard and fast, and this time Jackson thought the sensation was more than a threat.

Phone in his fist, he pressed it to his forehead as he leaned elbows to knees and gripped a fistful of hair. Never in his life. Just...never!

He'd been frustrated with his run—didn't make the time he'd wanted. Was upset that Sean hadn't been there—because if Sean had been there, Jackson was pretty sure they'd have both run a sub-three. They'd both have qualified for Boston, which might prove to his family two things: he didn't need their pity, because his life had long since moved on, and he was more than just a funny man who had an electrician's side gig to pay the bills. He was a grown-up—one they could take seriously every now and then. One who could do grown-up things.

Like marry a total stranger in Vegas.

God, forgive me!

What had he done?

**

Mackenzie lay perfectly still, inhaling the mixed scents of industrially cleaned linens, hints of her own lagging deodorant, and a subtle yet distinct aroma of manly-ish foresty cologne. She squeezed her eyelids tighter.

This was not real.

Couldn't be real.

If she just stayed still for a minute—no breathing, no peeking, no moving whatsoever—she would open her eyes and find herself...not there.

The boom of her heart, which made her pulse feel like the staccato rhythm of a snare drum throbbing through her body, demanded more air. Helplessly complying, she gulped in another breath.

His scent was still there.

She blinked against the sheets pressed to her face. Slowly peeled them back, desperately—and with a touch of delusion—hoping that the scene had miraculously changed.

It had not.

There she was, in the middle of a king-sized bed, in a Vegas Strip honeymoon suite, with a cold metal ring chilling her left hand. With a cautious eye on the bathroom door, she sat up. Smashing her hand into her thick, hard-to-tame waves, panic enclosed her body. Heart hammered. Lungs filled and emptied in rapid-fire beats. Throat clenched.

Mother would kill her. Right after she'd recovered from paralyzing shock. Her daughter, whom she'd raised to be entirely independent and with a deeply ingrained never-trust-a-man mentality, had married a man *she'd never met* until the night before.

Married!

She drew in a shaky, desperate breath.

Married!

Sliding her feet against the sheets, she drew her knees up and pressed her head against them.

What had she been thinking? She shouldn't even be in Vegas. She should be at home, safely sulking about her less-than-acceptable MCAT score. To think, the day before her biggest worry in life had been how to tell Mother that yet again she hadn't made the cut. Once again she wouldn't be attending the David Geffen School of Medicine at UCLA.

Yesterday that seemed like the worst news ever. How simple her life had been.

Now?

This was a *real* disaster.

The door across the room rattled, and before she could fling the sheets over her head and hope that her husband—Jack? No, Jackson... Jackson something with an M—Jackson emerged from the steam-filled bathroom.

Mackenzie ducked back to the mattress and held her breath again. What was he doing? If he slid into the bed beside her, she'd bolt.

Nothing. She couldn't even hear him breathing.

How had this happened?

Last night when he'd come across the crowded room, his eyes locked on hers. It had been magnetic. She'd walked into the club feeling entirely out of place. Like snow in Death Valley. Nearly drowning in self-consciousness, she'd followed Alyssa past the entry, reluctantly stepping deeper into the chaos of flashing lights, throbbing music, and constant chatter. Uncomfortable with everything about that moment—from her shoes to her dress to the fact that she regretted agreeing to this last-minute let's-forget-our-sorrows weekend—she'd slid the rogue hair from her eyes and glanced over the many faces within the loud space.

That was when it had happened. Her gaze snagged on him—dark hair, thick eyebrows, and brown eyes. He'd had a boy-next-door look: clean cut and a little bit out of place in this noisy, cut-loose, anything-goes crowd. He'd been frowning, maybe even brooding, but after their gazes had held for two breaths, the corners of his mouth hitched. That smile...charming, warm, and unique because of a scar that ran from the base of his nose through his top lip.

Something deliciously crazy had happened in her chest, and when he'd picked his way across the room toward her, she'd forgotten how much she didn't want to be there. She'd forgotten about the way she dreaded telling her mother about the MCAT scores and the way she dreaded even more another year of tutors and studying and frustration.

"Hi," he'd said.

"Hey." She'd been all breathy and ridiculous. But kind of liked it.

"I'm Jackson."

"Mackenzie."

He bought her a drink. Had one of his own. Then another...

He'd seemed nice. Safe. They laughed. Had fun.

How on earth had they ended up like this?

All she could remember was that she liked being with him. He was funny and had a rich, full laugh. He was nice to her. She found that grin of his thrilling.

And they'd had *a lot* to drink.

Still clutching the sheet, she felt the end of the bed move. As if a startled bunny, she scrambled away from the weight of him sinking into the mattress, feet sliding against the sheets, hands shifting and arranging to be sure she didn't reveal anything that shouldn't be seen.

Like that mattered now.

Dressed in dark jeans and a red T-shirt, he sat on the end of the bed. His shoulders—built like a man who worked outside an office or one who went to the gym after the office—rounded as he leaned against his legs. The chill of the headboard seeped into her back as she pressed away from him, wondering what he'd do. For several breaths, he stared at something—or nothing—across the large room. Then after a long draw of air, he turned to her, clearly forcing himself to meet her eyes.

"Hey." Discomfort ribboned his soft voice.

She cleared her throat. "Hi," she croaked.

One corner of his mouth tried to climb, as if he felt maybe a smile might help but couldn't manage it.

"Uh...so..." One hand left his leg and plowed through his damp hair. "Um, I think we..."

She glanced at the ring, then, with her fingers trembling, she held up her hand. "Yeah."

He looked at the ring, back at her face, then toward his feet.

Even breathing felt awkward. The silence that filled the room smothered them. After several moments of her watching the strong thud of his pulse move against his T-shirt, and feeling her own pound with equal strength, he shifted toward her again.

"I'm not sure what happened, Kenz."

Kenz? Had he called her that all night?

"I've never done anything so st—" He swallowed, cutting the word short. "I've never done anything like this." His eyes found hers again, a mix of alarm and sorrow making him seem more boy than man.

She shut her eyes, because looking at him stirred that crazy, good feeling in her again—and apparently that was a bad thing, considering where she'd landed. *What would Mother do?* Mother would kill her, that was what.

No, what would Mother do about this problem, if it were her?

She'd fix it and move on. No big deal. People did dumb stuff in Vegas all the time. But *what happens in Vegas...*

"We can fix this." The cut, dry tone in her voice surprised even her. But she kept a chilled, all-business expression as she looked at him. The way his eyes pinched—as if her statement made things worse, not better, messed with her confidence.

"The thing is, Kenz, I'm not the kind of guy who—"

She cut him off with a sharp laugh. "Marries a stranger in Vegas?"

His lips pressed closed.

"I'm not the kind of woman who marries at all." She straightened her shoulders, tugged at the ring on her finger, and when it was free, she held it across the space between them. "This was probably expensive—it looks real. But this marriage is not. Just something dumb we did because we both had too much to drink."

He stared at the ring, jaw clenched.

She leaned forward, took the hand closest to her, and pressed the diamond into his palm. "I'll take care of the paperwork. Leave me an address, and I'll get it to you as soon as possible."

Slowly, his fingers curved over the ring. Then clenched. When he met her eyes again, there was something fierce—maybe angry—lit there.

"Right," he said. "Just like that."

"Well, yeah. Just like that. Not a whole lot different than last night, don't you think?"

His jaw shifted hard again. "Exactly."

"You're from California, right?"

"We live in the same town. I do remember that."

"Should make things simple then," she said.

He stood, pocketed the ring, and looked down at her. The fire dwindled from his eyes, leaving only a soft echo of regret. "That's perfect, Kenz. I'll leave my information on the dresser."

"Good." She wanted him to leave. Couldn't handle the way his gaze made her feel...whatever it was she felt. He was just a drunken mistake. She didn't owe him anything. In fact, he should be thanking her, relieved that she was taking care of this without any sort of battle. Not looking at her as if this less-than-twelve-hour-relationship was actually a relationship at all. As if this hurt.

It didn't.

He checked his pockets. Wallet. Cell phone. Ring. Wrote something on the pad of paper on the dresser—likely his number. Hopefully, his last name too. That would help. Then he moved to the door.

"Kenz?" His hand rested on the handle, his body turned to leave, but his gaze settled on her.

"What?"

"I'm sorry."

With that, her *husband* walked out of the room.

Mother would never have to know.

Chapter Two
(in which Jackson and Mackenzie have problems)

Will I meet your wife next week?

Jackson stared at the screen. Connor hadn't said much since Thanksgiving weekend. Since Jackson had gone and gotten himself married. Of his six brothers, Jackson was closest to Connor. He'd sort of expected Connor to show up on his doorstep the morning after he'd returned to California from his Vegas fail.

Didn't happen.

Nor had he seen or heard from Mackenzie. Who was still his wife, because he hadn't seen any papers saying otherwise.

The phone in his palm buzzed again.

You're coming, right? Mom can't wait to meet your bride.

Great. That was fantastic.

Jacob and Kate are driving down from Seattle. That should be interesting.

Even better.

He could opt out. Not go. Spin a tale about spending the Christmas holiday with his wife's family. Because he was off to such a stellar start, why stop lying now?

We could drive up together. I could stop on my way and pick you cute lovebirds up.

No. Definitely not.

Hello?

Jackson glared at the phone. Connor wasn't usually a pest. What had gotten into him?

Forget it. He had wires to run. A house to light up. A life to sort out. He shoved his phone into his back pocket, only to have it buzz again.

With a growl, he whipped it to his face, expecting another peck from his younger brother.

Not this time.

Hello Jackson. This is Mackenzie Thornton. I'm going to assume you remember me and not feel the need to say that currently I'm your wife. However, I've attained the paperwork necessary to fix that problem. Just need your signature and we'll be on our way to safely annulled and free of all the stupid things said and done in Vegas. Let me know where to send the papers.

Jackson drew up his shoulders, which were taking on wooden-hanger stiffness. He'd married that? Sheesh. She sounded like an automated caller—the kind that pestered anyone and everyone about extending their car warranty, whether they owned a vehicle or not.

What a...

Another text vibrated the phone. Great fireballs, he was the Grand Central Station of texts today.

What do you say, brother? You are going to bring your wife home for Christmas, right? Mom deserves something here since you didn't bother to invite us to your wedding.

Where had this version of Connor come from? Jackson groaned, slumping against the pillar supporting the front porch of the house he was supposed to be wiring with Sean, and then sank to the step. Hand digging into his freshly cropped hair, he squeezed the phone.

Think.

Show up at home wifeless. Explain the whole sordid tale and spend Christmas with the sense that he was still a damaged child, still pathetic, and now also a huge disappointment. Or stay home, claim he was going to his in-laws for the holiday, and still feel childish, pathetic, and like an absolute failure.

Or...

Or.

Bad idea, Jackson...

No, it would work. It'd buy him some time. Give him a chance to figure out how to break the fall. And at least he wouldn't have to spend another Christmas with the Jacob-Kate-Jackson mess making everything weird.

He lifted the phone again, this time ready to type.

Hello Mackenzie. My wife. Where should we meet?

The little dots at the bottom of the screen rolled.

We don't need to meet. I just need your signature. The mail works fine.

He shook his head, mouth set with determination.

No. We need to talk. Friday. Pick a place downtown. I'll be there at seven.

***

Mackenzie stared at the ring Jackson had just plunked down on top of the paper. "Are you out of your mind?"

"Nope. It's one week. That's all I'm asking for. Then I'll sign your papers."

"Absolutely not." She snapped her attention back up to the man across from her. Gone were the boyish, regretful eyes of the Jackson who had walked away in Vegas. The one who had apologized. The one who had seemed as uncomfortable and horrified at their drunken stupidity as she had been.

This Jackson had locked-jaw determination set on his face. The fire she'd glimpsed back at the honeymoon suite was set to full-on blaze in his stare.

"I'm not signing then." He lifted a brow, as if to punctuate his stubborn position.

She crossed her arms, her shoulders stiff. "I don't actually need your signature to petition for an annulment, Jackson."

"No?" Now both brows lifted in challenge.

"No."

She had looked into it. An annulment didn't require both parties to petition. But he would have to sign in agreement at some point. Not to mention, if he didn't cooperate, it would take longer. Also, not to mention, it might be more likely to be denied without both petitions, depending on who was looking at the paperwork and how they interpreted *mentally incompetent or unable to understand what they were consenting to.*

In her estimation, *completely drunk* fell neatly into that provision. However, the lawyer had explained—quite flatly—that "we got drunk and made a mistake" is not legally a valid reason for an annulment, and judges were known to put the idiots who do such a dumb thing through the fire. "And," he'd said in an equally dry tone, "this is not my first rodeo with this situation. If the husband will sign on the front end, this will go much more smoothly and timely."

That conversation had been nearly as pleasant as this one.

Arms crossed, Jackson leaned his elbows on the table and bent toward her. "Your silence is telling, Mrs. Murphy."

"Don't call me that."

"You are my wife."

"Not for long."

"Gonna take a whole lot longer to undo the wife thing if I don't sign these papers, isn't it?"

Of all the pigheaded... Mackenzie growled. No wonder her mother had told her that marriage was a disaster and smart women stayed out of it.

Jackson sat back, his inhale a long draw, and then his hands fell to his lap. "Look, Kenz, I'm not meaning to be a jerk here."

"Oh really? You're accidently being one quite well."

The fire in his eyes dimmed again, allowing her to glimpse the much gentler—and regretful—man she'd remembered. He slid his phone across the table. "I need you to watch this."

After he tapped the screen twice, a video played.

Her stomach rolled. Good grief. They were ridiculous. Happy in that moment, but so completely ridiculous. How could Alyssa stand there as her witness, letting her go through with such a dumb idea?

She'd asked her roommate that. Alyssa had shrugged, as if the question was dumb. "You seemed happy, Mackenzie. I don't think I'd ever seen you so happy. Not stressing about school or work or your mother. And he was a really nice guy. Like, super nice. I kind of thought it was the most romantic thing I'd ever seen."

No, it was the dumbest thing she'd ever seen. Mackenzie had pointedly clarified that.

But watching the video...well, maybe Alyssa sort of possibly had a point. Mackenzie looked happy, and Jackson...

Even sitting there infuriated with the man across from her, when she studied the way he was with her in that video, well, if he wasn't a man completely smitten, he should have won an Oscar.

Yes. For sure, the man deserved an Oscar.

Maybe all actors were drunk on set?

The video ended, and she slid his phone back across the table. "That's lovely. Irrelevant, but lovely. At least now I can remember my wedding day."

"I sent it to my brother."

"What?"

"My brother has seen it. He told my family that we're married."

"Why did you do that?"

"Why did we get married?" He shook his head, palms pressing upward in the air. "I was drunk. I have no idea. I woke up that morning to a slew of texts from him, and yesterday he told me that"—he held up his fingers for air quotes—"'Mom can't wait to meet your wife.'"

She blew out a disgusted chuckle. "Sounds like you've got problems."

His face shifted to concrete. "*We've* got problems."

After a two-second stare-down, she slumped against the back of the chair. He seemed to take it as resignation.

"Here's the deal, wifey. You come up to Sweet Pine with me for Christmas—as my happily married, sick-in-love-with-me wife. After the week's up, we come back here, and I sign your papers."

"So dishonesty is a thing with you."

"Don't get off topic. And we are married, so..."

Mackenzie glared at the madman across from her. "You want me to act sick in love?"

"With me."

She rolled her eyes. "Oh, I'll be sick, all right."

"Nope. You'll be charming. And in love." He pinned a stiff look on her and then sipped his Coke. "Or you'll be stuck with me until the backed-up-to-the-moon divorce courts have time to deal with our drunken mistake."

"This farce is supposed to last a whole week?"

He cocked his brow like he thought she was being a child.

"What about my family?" Mackenzie said. "What am I going to tell my mom about not showing up for Christmas?" In her case, it wasn't a real argument. She could tell Mother she was working, and Mother would applaud her ambition. Christmas wasn't exactly a thing with them anyway. But Jackson didn't know any of that.

"Tell them you're spending the week with your new husband's family."

Mackenzie drew back, as if he spat poison. "I'm not telling my mother that I married a stranger in Vegas."

"Huh." His face read all smug satisfaction. "So dishonesty is a thing with you?"

"You're not funny."

He crossed his arms. "My paycheck from working stand-up gigs would say otherwise."

The punk actually got paid to act like this? Go figure.

"What about later?" Mackenzie asked. "Won't your family question such a fast divorce? Why even bother?"

"My problem, not yours. Right now, we're dealing with Christmas." His brows lifted, as if daring her to argue.

"Has anyone told you you're manipulative?"

"Not once."

"You are. And a jerk."

Scarlet splotched his neck, and he let his attention fall to the table. With total puzzlement, she watched while he battled himself. She could actually see the war between jerk and decent human playing out in the flinch of his expression.

Surprisingly, he shook his head. "I know."

He knew? That he was a jerk? That happened never.

With a side glance, he met her eyes. "Please, Kenz? I could really use this right now."

"Why?"

He answered her with silence.

Still slouched against her chair, the slider and fries he'd bought her waiting to be eaten, she let herself envision going to Jackson's family home for Christmas. Six brothers? She couldn't imagine. The house would likely be bursting and loud and busy...

Putting that up next to her normal holiday of mostly just her own company, suddenly the thought had a strange appeal. Like the kind of appeal people had for reality shows where one had to survive with nothing but a knife, a gun, and their wits. One didn't actually want to live that way, but maybe snagging just a glimpse of it...

"Okay." The word came out as a sigh. And a surprise.

To them both.

***

Mackenzie (text to Jackson): *I don't know how you hypnotized me into this insane scheme, but I've come to my senses. I'm out.*

Jackson: *Have fun petitioning for an annulment without me. My sources predict a 30% chance of success, after at least a 3 month wait. After the likely fail, you'll have to file for divorce. Want to take a stab at the wait on that?*

Mackenzie: *You're a bully.*

Jackson: *I'm offering you an idealistic Christmas trip to one of the most beautiful holiday-loving towns not in a Thomas Kinkade painting. It's actually very generous of me.*

Mackenzie: *You're also pompous.*

Jackson: *Not on a regular basis.*

Mackenzie: *Says you.*

Jackson: *You married me, princess.*

Mackenzie: *Not sober. Never, when sober. And don't call me princess.*

Jackson: *I don't remember you being this snarky.*

Mackenzie: *Do you even remember my last name?*

Jackson: *Murphy.*

Jackson: *Mrs. Murphy*

Jackson: *Princess Murphy*

The next morning...

Jackson: *Morning wife.*

Afternoon...

Jackson: We're still married.

Evening...

Jackson: *I can keep this up indefinitely.*

Mackenzie: *I can block your number.*

Jackson: *You'll have to talk to me at some point. Because, married. Princess.*

Mackenzie: *I'm working on that disaster.*

Jackson: *So I've heard. Could be a long year. Like I said, I can keep this up. Doesn't bother me one bit.*

Mackenzie: *Stalker.*

Jackson: *Married.*

Jackson: *I'll pick you up on Friday. 5:00 PM. It's a 2 1/2 hour drive. No silent treatment, it doesn't become you. Also, we're going to have to get to know each other for this to work. So bring your pleasant self that I vaguely remember.*

Mackenzie: *I told you I was out.*

Jackson: *So you want to stay married?*

Mackenzie: *You make me crazy.*

Jackson: *Crazy looks good on you.*

Mackenzie: *You can't even see me.*

Jackson: *I will. On Friday.*

Chapter Three
(in which Jackson takes his new wife home)

Man, there was something wrong with him. Why was he doing this? He wasn't sure he wanted to. Knew for a fact that she didn't want to. And yet here he was, pulled up to the curb of her townhouse, plowing forward into this idiotic plan, making Kenz crazy—and worse, making her think he was weird-crazy—in the process.

What was his deal?

He could call it off. Sign the papers. Head up toward the mountains alone and face his mistakes like a man.

The thought settled. It was what should be done. Inhaling the crisp December air as he walked up the sidewalk toward Kenzie's front door, Jackson worked to grip that resolve. Nearly had it in hand until her door flung open, and the woman he'd been antagonizing with names like *wifey* and *princess* stared him down with fire lighting her amber eyes.

And it happened. This he remembered—this connection that mysteriously gripped him deep in the gut. His heart stalled. An electrical current flashed through his whole body. And those thoughts about signing papers went up in flames.

"Ready to go, wife?"

He could almost hear the crackle of blazes in that look and had to work to keep the corners of his mouth tucked in.

"Ground rules first," she said.

"Are you insinuating that I'm not house trained?"

She crossed her arms. "I highly doubt it."

"I can be a perfect gentleman."

One lovely eyebrow arched into her forehead, beckoning him forward. Oh, so much fun... With slow, measured steps, he took the first riser to the entry, and then the second, which placed him directly in her space. The pulse in her neck thumped harder, and the sight of it throbbing nearly drew his touch.

"Bet," he said in a low tone.

"Bet what?" She held his gaze with a stubborn look, but her voice was breathless.

"I'm housebroken." He bent, the move drawing him so close that he could feel her breath fan against his chin. Which meant he knew when she held it. "A perfect gentleman."

She rolled her lips together.

Slowly, deliberately holding her wide-eyed stare, he reached for the bag at her feet and then straightened. Her shoulders sagged as he vacated the narrow, crackling space between them, and an almost irresistible warm pink splotched her freckled pale skin.

He held out his hand, palm up. "Shall we, wife?"

"Stop calling me that," she said, not a shred of conviction in the demand.

"Kenz." He winked. "Is that better?"

She eyed him, looking somehow stunned, irritated, and pleased at the same time.

"Than *wife*? Yes." She glanced down to his hand, straightened her posture, and then stomped down the sidewalk. "Let's get this over with."

He was being a pain, and he knew it. Man, but the fire though. He did like that fire.

***

It was like he possessed a twilight zone within his stare. She connected with him through those light-brown eyes, and suddenly she couldn't remember her name. Thornton, for the record. Her last name was Thornton. No matter what some marriage certificate from the state of Nevada said.

That seemed to be an issue she needed to keep clear in her head, because Jackson had charm. In spades. When he'd said to be prepared to talk, she'd taken a combat stance. He quickly disarmed her with stories about his family, his six brothers, and his penchant for pranks.

Who knew prank stories were so funny? Maybe it was just him—the way he delivered them. But when he storied his antics, she found herself not only relaxing, but actually smiling. Chuckling.

"You actually covered the toilet bowl with Saran wrap, and you'd never even met her before?" A horrified sort-of laughter bubbled from Mackenzie's chest.

Jackson flashed her a triumphant grin.

"What if she didn't have a sense of humor?"

"Then she would definitely not be a good match for Matt."

"Why? Is he as much trouble as you?"

"Trouble? I am absolutely no trouble at all, wife. I am fun. Pure fun."

He winked, and Mackenzie worked to cut off the thrill she felt at his flirtatious demeanor.

"Is Matt as much *fun* as I am? No contest. Matt's way more serious."

"Hmm." She attempted an unimpressed tone. Hoped it was successful. "And she married your brother anyway."

"Pretty sure that weekend sealed the deal. We Murphys are quite the irresistible bunch."

At that, she couldn't withhold her amusement. Clearly, Jackson could bewitch a crowd. "You're good at the stand-up gig, aren't you?"

With a lopsided grin that made the scar on his lip some kind of sexy, he shot her a look. "Not enough to pay the bills, hence the real job as an electrician. But I get a few laughs. Seven boys in one house makes for a minefield of material."

Everything from fake poop (ew. What a waste of chocolate, peanut-butter, and powdered sugar) to convincing one of his younger brothers that he'd turned him invisible—which apparently ended with a few tears and a lesson in how far is too far. Jackson had mischief turning around in his head more than anyone she'd ever met.

She'd gained enough backstory on him to know that two of his brothers were also married. He didn't say much more about any of his brothers in particular, except Jacob, who apparently didn't appreciate the pranks. When they were older elementary kids, Jackson had hid between the wall and Jacob's bed and waited until Jacob had settled in for the night. Then he brushed a feather across his brother's neck, holding back a snicker every time Jacob tried to swat at what he thought was a spider. When Jackson couldn't hold back any longer, he'd jumped from his hiding place and tackled his older brother. Jacob was livid. Didn't talk to Jackson for a week. After that, Jackson avoided pranking Jacob. No Saran wrap on the toilet for that brother's fiancée. No pepper in the saltshaker trick. No prank calls. Not with Jacob.

Still, Jacob had yet to get over it.

When their oldest brother, Matt, had married and Jackson not only decorated the outside of the car with the traditional mess, but also packed the inside with helium balloons and covered every conceivable surface from the steering wheel to the mirrors and the glovebox with athletic gauze pre-tape, Jacob glared at him and said, "You ever do this to my car and you're dead to me."

He'd totally meant it. Good thing Jacob had already been married by then.

"Why?" Mackenzie asked.

Jackson shrugged, his jaw clamping a little tighter. "Doesn't think it's funny, I guess. Like I said, Jacob is a little...different. But then again, I'm different, too. We're just opposite kinds of different."

"Will Jacob be there this week?"

"We'll all be there this week."

Jackson also managed to pull her out of her shield of silence—a shield that she used in all of life, not just with him. She was the compliant type. The try-to-please-those-in-charge type. The I-don't-like-conflict type.

He'd raised an eyebrow at that. Because with him, she had some flare. An anomaly that she wasn't sure what to make of and was a little bit afraid to think too much about.

"Tell me something quirky about yourself," he'd asked when she'd stayed clammed up too long.

That required thought. Mackenzie figured she was painfully average. No quirks. None to be impressed with, anyway. Not like being a part-time stand-up comedian.

Finally, something came to mind. Not much—rather stupid—but it was all she had. "I love new socks. I'd wear a new pair of socks every day if I could."

"Never a used pair again?"

A tiny chuckle parted her lips. "If I could."

He seemed oddly delighted with that, and the conversation rolled on from there.

By the time he pulled up to a large log home tucked off a curvy mountain road among a forest of evergreens, she'd shared that she was an only child, and it was just her and her mother, and that she had a degree in human biology, had studied premed, and worked at the lab in the hospital as a phlebotomist.

"Don't be too impressed," she'd said when he blew a low whistle. "I draw blood. That's my job. It's not nearly as fascinating as the title. Spelling it, in fact, is way more interesting."

"But premed..."

"Yeah, well, you still have to get into med school."

The glance he cast toward her was both serious and sympathetic, and she got the impression he remembered some of that story from their time in Vegas. Feeling overexposed, she raised that shield of silence again.

For the moment, he let her hide behind it, choosing stillness himself. Gazes fixed beyond the windshield at the house covered with garland and strung up with white LED lights, it seemed that together they drew a long breath.

"Ready for this?" he asked, the serious version of the man overshadowing the confident goofball he'd been on the drive up.

The warm, gentle sincerity in his eyes, now settled on her, puddled warmth in her chest. "You'll be a gentleman?"

"Promise. You'll be sick in love?"

"I've never been sick in love."

"Now's your chance to try it out."

She smirked. Couldn't help it, because though he was annoying with this, he was also sort of cute.

He leaned closer, and she inhaled a breath of that piney forest scent that she remembered of him. Lifting her hand, he slid the ring back onto her finger. "With me."

"What?"

"You're sick in love with me." His lips brushed her knuckles, and then he dropped another wink.

She should be completely irritated.

**

Jackson stared across the backyard, tension rippling his back muscles enough that she could see it through his dark T-shirt. Yeah, all that laughter in there had been a cover-up. It bothered him.

"Did you really run the Vegas marathon?"

He glanced over his shoulder at her approach, expression a little like he'd been caught. Mackenzie crossed the deck and leaned her backside against the railing, next to him. She waited while he studied her. There was snap in his eyes, more evidence of the emotion he'd kept fairly well hidden while in there with his family. Slowly he straightened, reached to his back pocket, and brought out his phone. He scrolled without a word. Ignoring her?

Man, this guy could go from decent person to jerk in record time. The drive up had been...well, if she was being honest, at some points, enjoyable. Jackson was funny. Quick with the jokes, his deep laughter something she remembered liking about him when they'd first met.

But this switch to brooding...good grief. She had enough moody in her life. Certainly didn't need it from her real-not-real husband.

Okay, well, the guys in there did harass him something fierce.

Not that he shouldn't expect it—especially since he was the self-proclaimed family clown. After all, he'd wasted absolutely no time duct taping several phones, chargers, and a Chromebook to the ceiling in a bedroom, later shouting with laughter when one of the high school brothers yelled loud enough to hear from anywhere in the house.

But when he'd told the family why he was in Vegas—during the much-anticipated story of how Jackson and Mackenzie met—they'd howled. Mocked brutally.

"The Vegas marathon, Jackson?" One of the many brothers that she hadn't yet straightened out in her mind had jeered. "Weren't you the one who puked after the Sunset Mile in ninth grade?"

The gang of boys had laughed. Kept poking him with their doubt.

"You used to stop halfway down the driveway when Mom would send us out because we were driving her nuts. Said you were a sprinter, not a distance runner, and you might were gonna die if you had to run the full block."

"Didn't you join track so that you could hang out with that distance runner? What was her name? Anyway, soon as she found out you couldn't even last an eight hundred, she was done with you. Remember that?"

Jackson had chuckled through it. Faked good sport really well. But she'd heard the difference in his laugh. It'd gone shallow.

So she'd followed him out to the deck. For pity's sake. Now he was ignoring her. Because he'd got his feelings hurt? How on earth was a guy like this that sensitive?

When she was ready to give up, walk away with a huff out of this excessively loud house and away from this sham of a marriage she'd managed to get tangled up in, he flipped the screen toward her.

The man in the picture was the man she'd married. Though he looked much more serious in that shot than she'd seen from him with his family—present moment being an exception. And wow, that was a lot of sweat. His shirt looked soaked, his shoulders glistened under the Strip's neon lights, and his thick dark hair was plastered to his head. Behind him was a *Congratulations, Finishers! You did it!* sign.

"Wow. You did it."

"Yeah. Great." Jackson's mouth flattened as he clicked the Home button and shoved the phone back into his pocket. "Even my wife is shocked."

"Um, well. I don't actually know you, so..."

He glanced over his shoulder.

"Don't worry. It's just us out here," she said.

Turning back to face the yard, Jackson leaned his forearms against the deck rail. His shoulders rounded as he faced the woods beyond the manicured grass.

"How'd you do?" Kenzie asked, not sure why she was interested. Except seeing the guy who she thought was carefree and thoughtless get pummeled the way he had in there bothered her. Did his brothers know this side of Jackson? Did they ever see that their dismissal of him as anything serious upset him?

"Three hours, ten minutes. About." His head dipped farther down, curving his shoulders more.

"That sounds pretty awesome."

"Thanks. It's not what I was shooting for though."

"What were you shooting for?"

"Sub-three."

Her eyebrows pinched. "I don't know what that means."

"Three hours or less. Preferably less. I'd done it a couple of times before, in training."

"But ten minutes. I mean, that's not bad. And you finished, right? You ran a whole freaking marathon. Have any of your brothers run a whole freaking marathon before?"

Jackson shrugged. "Doesn't matter."

She crossed her arms and waited for him to explain the disappointment he clearly felt.

"A sub-three would have qualified me for the Boston marathon. That was the goal. Why I started running in the first place."

"But you said you've done it before."

"Right. In training. Not in a race. You have to qualify in a recognized race before you can enter the Boston. And I can't afford to keep going around the country trying to do something that I clearly can't do. So."

"Oh."

Jackson ran a hand over his head, making that dark hair stand on end.

"Why didn't you show that picture to your family?"

He stood straight again, braced his hands on the railing, and arched backward. "Not worth it."

"What do you mean?"

His gaze fell on her, the study in his eyes intense. As if gauging whether or not she'd be worth sharing his explanation with. Unexplainably, she hoped he'd confide in her. Didn't make sense, that quiet yearning she felt, but it was there, hoping he'd share this little sliver of himself with her.

"You know *Snow White and the Seven Dwarfs?*"

"Um, I know the Disney version. Does that work?" An oddity of her childhood. Disney in general had been forbidden, as her mother had believed that they only ever taught girls to be pretty, sing happy, and wait for a man to make them complete. She'd only seen a few—*Snow White* being one—because she'd watched them at a friend's house and had never told her mother about it.

"Perfect. Each dwarf has a name that corresponds with who they are, right?"

"Right."

"So in my family, I'd be Dopey."

"Always?" She shouldn't be surprised, prankster that he was. But she'd only known him for less than a month and had spent less than two full days with him, and she could see he was layered. Surely his family knew that too.

"Always." His tone was dark and flat. Defeated.

Mackenzie watched while the lowering sun caught the glossy black of his hair and highlighted a subtle ache in his eyes. She was certain very few ever glimpsed this side of him. Honestly, she got why he'd get tagged with Dopey. He wasn't serious. Goofy 90 percent of the time. Came off as if fun was the ultimate goal in life. Not to mention irresponsible. After all, who got married to a total stranger in Vegas?

Um. Well.

She dropped her gaze to her shoes.

But Jackson? He fit the type who would, even if she didn't, on a regular basis. He was impulsive. Ridiculous. Her absolute opposite in every way.

All reasons she knew that Jackson Murphy was not husband material. Not that she had husband material in mind. She'd been trained to not need one. Ever. The sum of it? They were all reasons she intended to file for an annulment as soon as possible after this coerced visit with his family was over.

But this little revelation, that something actually bothered him, and it might explain a few things about the guy she didn't mean to marry? It burrowed in her heart. Pricked a tiny bit of compassion for the man who, for the past two weeks, had become the bane of her existence.

"Now you have me figured, don't you, Miss On-Her-Way-to-Med-School?"

The barb in his voice stung, and she looked up, ready to deliver her own dart. But through the window of the French doors leading to the deck, she caught sight of two of Jackson's younger brothers. Both animated, they gestured toward her and Jackson, laughed, and then smacked hands together like they were settling on a bet.

About them—their marriage?

She wasn't sure why the pity she felt for him surged so strong or why she felt the heat of anger at his brothers to the degree that she did. But both roiled in her gut. Pushing off the railing, she turned to face Jackson. With a step, she sidled in between his body and the deck railing, and his eyes widened when she reached to cup his jaw.

"Kiss me."

"What?" He leaned in, confusion wrinkling his forehead.

With her free hand, she tugged his T-shirt. The hand on his face slid to his neck. She pushed up, as if to take his mouth with hers, and whispered, "Your brothers are watching. We're newlyweds. So kiss me."

Then she closed the gap between them.

Jackson was stiff, his mouth hard. But she kissed him anyway. Suddenly his breath warmed her lips, a sigh eased the tension in his back and shoulders, and his hands slid around her. The pretend-we-actually-want-to-be-married kiss became convincing. To everyone.

For a few breathless moments, Mackenzie forgot all the reasons.

Chapter Four
(in which Mackenzie sleeps in a cold basement)

"You cannot be serious." Their kiss on the deck lingered in her memory, and maybe she wanted to hang on to it but wasn't admitting it. However, that lip action had not softened her up for this little bit of news.

"Completely." Jackson dropped an arm around her, fingers sliding on her hip as if that was where they belonged. "Surprise!"

Glaring up at him, she did *not* smile.

"It's kind of a tradition. The newest married couple gets the crappiest bed." He gripped the back of the couch and gave it a little shake. "So here we are."

She gripped the intruding hand upon her person, shoved it back into his gut, and spun to glare at him. "I have *never* in my life slept on anything that had *hide-a* in its formal title."

"How have you lived?" Amusement danced in his eyes.

"I'm not sleeping in the basement family room," she whispered furiously.

"It's the only available bed."

"Then call a hotel."

With two fingers, he pressed her lips together. "You're gonna hurt my mom's feelings. We don't do things like stay in a hotel during a family holiday. It just isn't done among the Murphys, my red-carpet wifey."

"Stop calling me that."

Jackson smirked, one eyebrow lifted, as if she'd just given him ammunition. "You're some kind of hoity-toity, aren't you?"

"I can't converse with a man who uses made-up words."

"Not made up, smarty-pants."

"Is so."

"Bet." He leaned closer, his laughing gaze dropping to her mouth.

Mackenzie ignored the zing in her stomach and stepped around him. "I'm calling a hotel."

He caught her forearm and leaned down. Mackenzie tried to ignore the way his piney scent curled around her, as well as the way her body responded to the warm breath that fanned against her jaw as he spoke.

"You do that, the deal's off," he whispered.

"What?"

He released his soft hold on her arm and turned her chin so that she'd look at him. And there he was. Right there. Noses nearly brushing. The moment felt a little bit like agony, especially when the memory of that kiss surged.

"In this house, for this week, you're my sick-in-love-with-me wife. That's the deal. Or no signing papers for this husband. You'll be stuck with me."

He was bluffing. Had to be bluffing. He didn't want to be stuck with her any more than she wanted to be stuck with him.

Yes. She obviously believed that. Explained perfectly why she'd agreed to this blackmail trip in the first place. Still, why would he want to stay married to her?

Oh, but that kiss...

The world seemed to shift around her, and for a moment she thought to reach out, to snag the front of his shirt for stability. Good grief, her mind was weak. Put a bit of chemistry between her and the Neanderthal, and she was mush.

Am not. She squared her shoulders, stared right back into his eyes. "You could have mentioned the hide-a-bed in the basement *family room* before we came," she hissed.

That easy, annoyingly confident smile lifted on his mouth. "I could have."

Lips pursed, she kept her glare leveled on him. He kept right on grinning.

"You know, your nostrils flare when you're mad."

The jerk. She wasn't going to back away from a jerk.

"Come to think of it"—he leaned to whisper in her ear again—"they flare other times too."

Heat flooded her face. With both hands on his solid chest, she pushed.

Jackson chuckled, patted her cheek, and moved away. "I'll be back in ten minutes, wifey."

Mackenzie growled. Ten minutes? Great. Ten minutes was all she had to get changed, brush her teeth, and force herself to be sound asleep before the prankster-driven caveman came back to join her on that stupid *hide-a-bed*.

How was this even fair? Shouldn't the newlyweds get the private bedroom instead of the couple who'd been married for longer than five minutes? This family was nuts. Which explained a whole lot about Jackson. He was crazy. He was driving her crazy.

She wasn't going to survive this.

Shutting her eyes, Mackenzie forced her erupting thoughts to slow. She'd survived a lot in life. Her mother's unattainably high expectations. The plans the woman had laid out for Mackenzie to endlessly strive after. Being the oddball all her life—the weirdo who didn't date and barely had friends. If she could persevere through all that, surely she could outlast the halfwit and his backwoods family for a week. She just needed to do the next thing. Conquer the next challenge.

Which would be putting on her jammies. Thinking about that about made her head explode, and she couldn't stop the curse from hissing under her breath. She'd brought boxer shorts and a tank top. That was it.

The Murphys' basement was freezing, and the blankets spread over the mattress--which appeared to be about as comfortable as a rice cake—weren't thick.

She was going to die.

No, she wasn't. She'd wear a pair of leggings that were supposed to go with a sweater tunic. And maybe the sweater too.

She could hear Jackson's mocking laughter already.

Okay, just the leggings. That'd be okay. The leggings and her tank top, and she'd wrap up in a blanket. That would do double duty—the blanket would be a shield between her and her stupid *husband*, in case he thought they were playing house for reals.

He didn't, right? Jackson wouldn't...

So she'd sleep wrapped up like a mummy, with her can of Mace.

"Welp." Jackson's voice drifted from the top of the stairs. "It's been fun. Good night, all."

Was that like a warning? Mackenzie shifted into panic-induced-frenzied speed. Her sweater and jeans landed in a crumpled pile on the floor—which was bound to keep her up all night because they weren't right side out and folded—and slipped her tank top over her head.

Oh my word, it's like the arctic in here!

Footfalls called a hollow notice on the steps. *The caveman cometh.* Never mind the cold. The leggings would help. She worked them over her feet. Wiggled, scraping them up over her legs. Why were these things so...

"Need help?"

No! Just...ugh. She commanded calm into her demeanor. Adjusted her crooked waistline. Turned, lifted her chin, and met his laughing eyes. Hands braced on her hips, she raised her eyebrows. "Not from you."

He laughed. She roiled. He was always laughing! Life was not that funny. *She* was not that funny.

"I need to brush my teeth." She spun to grab her overnight bag.

"That's a good idea."

She ignored his jab. "I assume you at least have indoor plumbing?"

He crossed his arms and gestured with his chin. "Past the stairs. On the right."

"Good."

"You're welcome." He chuckled as she passed.

The week was already long, and it hadn't even been twenty-four hours.

When Mackenzie came back to their "room," it was pitch black. She tried to conjure up a mental map of the space as she felt her way across the blackness. When she thought it was about the right distance, she turned. Her nose caught the cold, hard metal of the support post. "Ouch."

"Need help?"

She growled. "You're infuriating."

"No? Okay. Good luck."

"Jackson Murphy!"

"What? I offered."

"Turn on the lights so I can see where I'm going."

The sound of blankets and sheets shuffling provoked a cramp over her entire body. He was in bed. Their bed. The one they would share for a whole week.

A glow chased the darkness, coming from her right. He'd turned on his phone and was using it to direct her. Like she was an airplane.

"Better?" he asked, mischief in his tone.

"Why didn't you just leave the lights on?" She stepped away from the post she'd just nose kissed and around the couch-turned-bed of humiliation.

"This is so much more romantic."

"Oh, for the love of cats."

"I'm allergic to cats. Sorry."

She sat on the mattress, and it crackled. "What is that?"

"What?"

She shifted, emphasizing the crackling. "That. What is that sound?"

"Oh. The plastic cover. Mom put it on years ago when Brayden was little. He was a bed wetter."

"Omigosh!" She curled into a ball, shoulders pressed into her knees.

Jackson's low chuckle preceded more plastic crackling sound.

"Just kidding. Brayden never slept on the hide-a-bed. That I know of."

"This week is going to kill me."

"Nah. You'll be a better person for it."

She sat up, turned, and glared at him. If it weren't for that charming grin that puddled something warm in her belly, she might have slapped him.

He shifted more, sitting up. Thank goodness he was wearing a shirt. Dare she hope there were pants on under those blankets? Better be. His hand covered her shoulder and squeezed. "Lay down, Kenz. Go to sleep." He flipped back the blankets as a punctuation to his invitation. Or was it an instruction?

Heaven help her. But also, thank goodness, because yes, he wore pants. Sweats. Which looked much warmer than her thin leggings. Reminded of the frigid temps they were to dwell in, she shivered and scampered under the blankets and then remembered her plan about wrapping one around her. For warmth. And protection from the imp beside her.

The stupid imp had spread out all the blankets already.

With her back to him, she pressed her shoulder into the thin mattress. It gave with the sound of crackers under one's shoe and felt about as comfortable as a worn-out airplane seat. With the slightest click, the light from Jackson's phone vanished, and they were left in a cold, black togetherness.

Mackenzie squeezed her eyes shut. Commanded her mind to shut down. If she could go to sleep, this agony would end sooner. She'd have one day to mark off the calendar. One day gone, six to go.

The air bit her nose with a chill, and she tucked her face into her fist, which clutched a ball of the blankets. A shiver trembled through her.

"Jackson," she whispered.

"What?" He bit the word.

"It's freezing."

"No wonder. You're dressed like its summer in that tank top. What part about December in the mountains did you not understand?"

"My room at home does not feel like the North Pole. You should have warned me."

His sigh sounded a bit like a growl. The mattress beneath her swayed, crackling again like a wrapper being crunched as he moved. She rolled to her back, wondering if he was leaving her on her own. Which would be lovely. But he didn't get up.

Instead, something thick fell from the darkness onto her face. The fabric was chilly and smelled faintly like Jackson.

"Put it on," he said. "Should help."

His sweatshirt. Never before had she stooped to wearing a man's sweatshirt. When all the other girls in high school and college would run around in their boyfriend's oversized clothes, thinking they were adorable, she'd held on to her independent dignity.

But she'd never been trapped in a dark basement and shivering like a popsicle either. Or married, for that matter. Her mother would die. Possibly disown her because there she was, teetering on all that Mother had despised. A little wife, all smothered up in her big man's sweatshirt, set to be barefoot and pregnant in no time. Mackenzie couldn't even bring herself to tell Mother that she hadn't passed her MCAT and wasn't getting into medical school. How would she ever confess that she'd gotten married? In Vegas? While drunk?

Oh! How far she'd fallen. Oh! How Mother's head would explode.

"Kenz, if you're not going to wear that, I will."

Not a chance. Mother would never know any of this anyway. "I'm wearing it." Feeling for the tag, she slipped the bulk of it over her head and settled it around her body. She lay back down, burrowing into the blankets and the sweatshirt. It did smell like him. She buried her nose into the fabric and inhaled. Yes. Piney with a hint of citrus scent.

"Better?"

"I guess," she mumbled.

The crackling mattress sounded again, and Jackson's movement wiggled the entire bed. Before she understood that he wasn't just lying back down, one large arm hooked over her shoulder, tucked around her body, and his hand anchored on the shoulder she'd dug into the crunchy mattress.

Mackenzie froze. Body tight, she held her breath.

"Just relax." He tucked her under his chin and into his chest. "I'm not getting frisky. Just want you to warm up so you'll shut up. Then maybe I can go to sleep."

Charming.

Warmth seeped from his body into her back, and slowly the shivering stilled.

"Jackson?"

"What?" His voice rumbled low, as if he were drifting off and not up for a conversation.

"Why are we doing this?"

The arm around her tightened, and she felt his breath come and go. Other than that, nothing.

"Jackson?"

"Go to sleep, Kenz."

After that, he didn't mumble another word. His breath, warm in her hair, deepened and slowed, and the bundle of muscle surrounding her softened. When she was certain he'd drifted off, she let herself relax into him.

Warm. Held. She slipped into a sleep that was surprisingly comfortable, holding on to the secret she'd never tell her mother.

She rather delighted being swallowed in this man's arms.

***

Why were they doing this?

Jackson stared into the darkness, careful to keep his breathing slow, his body relaxed. Mackenzie had surrendered to sleep, her body soft as she allowed him to hold her. A minor miracle all by itself. Then again, she had kissed him earlier, even in his worst moodiness. So there was that.

He inhaled carefully, aware that his heart rate had jolted with the memory of that kiss. The warm scent of whatever flowery kind of shampoo or other hair nonsense she used filled him. If only this woman was like this when she was conscious and sober.

All warm and soft and...smellable.

Clearly he'd gone nuts.

All he'd had to do was sign the papers. Sign. The. Dang. Papers. This had to be the dumbest impulse he'd ever chased down in his life. Well, this and the whole marrying-a-stranger-in-Vegas thing. Why hadn't he just cooperated with the annulment? It was clean. Easy. Sign a statement saying they were both drunk, therefore were not in a state of mind to make responsible decisions. Certainly they wouldn't be the first rodeo when it came to this kind of situation, especially living so close to Vegas. The judge or whoever had to approve the annulment probably had a stamp all ready to go. One they used daily to legally undo all the stupid things that got done in Sin City.

All he'd had to do was cooperate. Instead...

Instead he was holding the woman who was currently his wife—a woman he barely knew—while they played happy newlyweds for his family. And liking the way she smelled.

All for what? Because he wanted his brothers to take something about him seriously? Because he was tired of the weirdness that continued to play out between Jacob, Kate, and himself? Because he didn't want the pity he could read like a digital clock in his mother's eyes? Yes. All those reasons.

He'd been fine. For a couple of years, he'd been fine. The whole Jacob/Kate gut punch healed, and he'd moved on. *They* still kept the weird going though, like they both thought he should be pining for the woman his big brother had swiped. His response? Bring home a fake-real wife. Brilliant. That should make everything not weird. And would definitely give him a solid spot in the family as something other than Dopey, the stand-up comedian.

With a long, controlled sigh, he shut his eyes. He should have talked to Sean about all this. Told him what had happened in Vegas. Asked for some serious advice. Typical Jackson move though. Just operate on impulse and hope for the best.

At least he'd have some material for new sets. No doubt the late-night crowds looking for a good laugh would find his strange, insane life hilarious. They'd rock back and forth, slap the tables, clap about his idiotic choices because it cracked them up, and the club would pay him. After which he could go home to his empty house, read something that would remind him he was a grown-up and could think about things more significant than Saran wrap on the toilet, then drift to sleep to the mind-numbing drone of an infomercial. The glam life of a stand-up comedian.

A lonely life. Truth be known, he felt the honesty of what his brothers seemed to think of him: he was pathetic.

Mackenzie sighed, her weight shifting so that she lay more against him than the crappy mattress he'd volunteered them to sleep on. She was warm and soft, and he liked the feel of her. Liked the smell of her. Liked the memory of her kiss.

Guilt slipped into that thought—and maybe the real reason he hadn't just signed those papers. He'd *married* this woman. Slept with her. Somehow it just didn't seem right to pretend it'd never happened.

He would always know that it had happened, and his life would never be the same.

Hey, God? Sean says You specialize in turning messes into a message. You got one for this?

No response. Jackson settled a little more comfortably, tucking the blankets around Mackenzie so that the chill wouldn't bother her, and moved his chin so that he could smell her hair. Slowly sleep nudged reality away, and as his thoughts slipped into the fuzzy place that wasn't always sensible, one whispered deep into his heart.

No. Life would never be the same. And he'd never regret it.

Chapter Five
(in which Jackson gets soaked)

Her first thought was that she could still smell him. She might have smiled a little, but to be fair, she was still mostly asleep. Her second, that he'd kept her warm, and her mother clearly had never experienced this before. Mackenzie definitely smiled then.

The third thought...

We're not alone.

Jarred, she sucked in a breath and her eyes flew open.

"Don't move." Jackson's breath tickled her ear as his gravely, low voice seeped into her hearing. "They think we're still asleep."

Against his instruction, she turned her chin to find his face in the dim light. As she shifted her gaze, she realized the lack of light had more to do with the blanket Jackson had secured over their heads than the lack of daylight that must have been filtering in from the egress window behind them.

Jackson's eyes met hers, the ever-present amusement in them. "I'm serious. Be still."

"Why?" she breathed.

"Because." Half a grin quirked his mouth. "Of the element of..." He flipped the blankets back and jumped to his feet on the bed. "Surprise!"

The moment the blanket left her person, pandemonium broke out. Shouts surrounded her. Battle cries. "Attack! Get them!"

"Take cover, Kenz!" Jackson lunged over the back of the couch, tackling one of his two younger brothers. Brayden maybe?

"What is happening?" Dazed and a little terrified, she watched dumbstruck while a flurry of motion whipped about her. Something whizzed by her ear. Another same something struck Jackson's exposed back and bounced to the floor.

"Reload!" one of the brother's shouted.

They were shooting? What were they shooting? What was this madness?

"Kenz, take cover!"

Jackson laughed, did some kind of kick sweep take-down thing, pinned Brayden to the floor, and then flew back onto the bed they'd shared. He snatched the blanket at her feet and flung it over their heads.

"What is happening here?"

"Are you kidding? We're under attack."

"Why?"

"Because I have brothers."

"That's a reason?"

A sound like elephants stampeding clamored on the stairway. Feeling horrified—what dignified human attacked a mostly-still-sleeping person in their sort-of bedroom?—Mackenzie studied Jackson.

"Don't freak out, okay?"

"What?"

"Don't go all hoity-toity on me and freak out. 'Kay?"

"Are you—"

"Attack! Full attack! Give no mercy! Take no prisoners!"

The blanket jerked and then was snatched away. Jackson gave her one pleading look and then lunged over her, covering her head with his arms, shielding her with his body. Popping sounds snapped from all around her. The boys continued to shout. Colorful, gooey string seeped through the gaps where Jackson's body couldn't protect her.

And then she understood. This was play. His brothers were...playing. Even though the youngest was seventeen. Even though she was in bed, in her pajamas, and a virtual stranger. It was bizarre. And yet something of it beckoned to her. A life she'd secretly wondered about.

The bed beneath her jostled as one of the boys tried to dislodge her husband. A can of something rolled on the crackling bed near her leg. She shifted to reach it and found the gooey string still attached to the nozzle.

The can felt mostly full. A smile moved on her lips. It felt...wicked. And fun.

She flung away the sheets entangling her legs. "Enough!"

Her hearty yell silenced the chaos. Jackson's eyes slid to her, horror rounding them. She bit her lip. She winked, and the laughter resettled in his gaze. As if a silent *now* had sounded between them, he tackled the brother on their bed and she sprang from the mattress, sliming whoever she could with the silly string as she ran from the basement, up the stairs, and out the back doors.

Footfalls pounded after her.

"Run, Kenz! Save yourself. Don't worry about me...your husband...who protected you..."

Jackson's dramatic shouts faded as she sprinted from the deck to the yard. Heart pounding, breath spent—more from laughing than from running—she spun to face her pursuers. Two grown men, who looked, to varying degrees, a bit like the man she'd come with to this home, closed ranks around her.

"You have spunk." One grinned.

Tyler, she thought, *two years younger than Jackson.*

"And good news—she's fast. Jackson won't be able to run when he's in trouble."

Conner. The one with the military cut was Conner. And he didn't know anything, because Jackson could outrun them all.

She held up her can of silly string. "Stay back, you beasts. Or I'll paint you ridiculous."

"There now," Tyler said, creeping nearer. "Be a nice sister-in-law and surrender the silly string."

The French door to the deck above popped open, and a rush of shouts and footfalls spilled onto the deck.

"Don't touch my wife!"

Mackenzie glanced up, finding Jackson dashing off the deck stairs, Brayden the baby brother wrapped like a monkey around his back, and another brother—the oldest?—close on his heels. He ran across the yard, barreled past the two who had surrounded her, and tossed Brayden onto the ground. In a breath, he was at her back, one arm possessively around her shoulders, the other extended with some kind of plastic gun pointed at the boys. His heart hammered against her back, labored breath puffing white into the chilly morning air.

"All right, boys," Helen Murphy stepped onto the deck, hands on her hips and laughter curling her mouth. "You've terrified my new daughter-in-law enough. Let them go."

"You know we can't do that, Mom," Connor answered. His eyebrows bounced a little, and he tried not to smile. "Protocol."

What did that mean?

A savage shout sounded behind her only a moment before something cold and wet flew at them from behind. Jackson pulled her in, curled himself around her, taking the bulk of whatever was dousing them.

"Brandon!" Jackson's hold tightened, and he shivered. "Oh, come on, guys! It's December!"

Laughter filled the yard.

"Very funny," Helen said, amusement in her voice. "Not one of you gets a warm shower today. Except, of course, Jackson and Mackenzie. Now stop acting like terrorists and leave them alone."

The boys disbanded. Mackenzie tried to straighten, though Jackson still held her. When she turned to him, she found he was soaked. She also found his arms still held her safe.

"You okay?" he asked.

"Yes. And apparently warmer than you are."

"Good thing you have my sweatshirt. I guess I got payback, didn't I?"

"Payback?"

"For not telling you about the basement."

She chuckled.

"Serious though." He rubbed her arms. "You okay? We're a wild bunch. Should have warned you about that too."

"Yes. I'm fine. This normal in your family?"

"Very. Sorry."

"Oh." A hollowness opened in her chest. A feeling of missing out. "Are...are you okay?"

"I'm good." He grinned, tucked her under one soaked arm, and walked her back to the house. He guided her up the deck, through the upstairs, and back down to the basement bathroom. "Take a warm shower."

"You should first. You're soaked."

He studied her, his eyes roaming over her face. "You're not what you think, are you, Kenz?"

"What?"

"Nothing." He nudged her into the bathroom. "Take your time. I'll get your bag."

***

The day swept by, calmer than it had started, until Jackson's last brother arrived at the house. Tall, dark hair, pressed designer clothing, and an overall sophisticated air foreign to the rest of the Murphy boys defined Jacob Murphy as he took over the living room upon his arrival. At his side, a petite blond woman hung on his arm. She appeared flawless. Long, silky hair, sparkling blue eyes, and dressed to impress—though Mackenzie couldn't imagine why. The group of them—sans Jacob and his wife, Kate, of course—had spent the day meandering through the woods cutting evergreen boughs for Helen, who would use them in the morning for her Christmas arrangements. Jacob and Kate, both individually and as a couple, struck an odd chord in this band of ruffians.

The couple were people Mackenzie might have normally gravitated toward. Something about that unsettled her.

"Jacob, you've made it." Helen rose from her spot on the sofa next to Kevin, Jackson's dad. "At last my gang of boys is all together again."

"Hello, Mother." Jacob moved to hug her, though his voice

and manners seemed stiff. Maybe pompous.

How was this man related to this crew? Specifically, to Jackson? If Jackson was the wild west, Jacob was English peerage. If Jackson was beer and chips, Jacob was champagne and caviar. If Jackson was flannel and jeans, Jacob was cashmere and silk. If...

Mackenzie stopped the mental comparisons, realizing that she stared at the couple who'd snatched center stage—blocking the football game the brothers had been watching.

Jackson leaned against her shoulder and whispered near her ear. "Shut your mouth. And please, *for the love of those cats*, don't drool."

She jerked away from the tickle of his breath. "What?"

Their eyes met at a glance, irritation in his. And a hint of disappointment? She couldn't know for sure. He stood, gripping her hand as he moved and squeezing her fingers, as if a silent plea.

"Jacob, old boy." Jackson mimicked a high-brow accent with the precision of a professionally trained actor. Did she detect an undertone of resentment? "How's the other side these days?"

Mackenzie followed him as he stepped across the space, and the room stilled. Eerie and full of warning. Like the calm before a storm. She glanced at Helen, who had hugged a stiff Kate and then stepped to the side of the couple.

"Jackson." Jacob grinned, rolling his shoulders straight. "Wondered if you'd be here."

"Why wouldn't I be?"

Kate swallowed. Her gaze pinned solely on Jackson. Worry and something else filled her wide eyes.

Stopping two steps from the other couple, Jackson pulled Mackenzie snug to his side. "This is Kenz." He looked down at her. Smiled. Studied her as if he adored every freckle on her face, the copper of her eyes, and the curve of her jaw. His gaze didn't leave her. "Mackenzie Thornton. Murphy."

No one said a word. Then, "Murphy?" Disbelief rather than shock rang through Jacob's response. In fact, it almost sounded like he'd laughed.

One corner of Jackson's mouth slid up a moment before he

squared to his brother again. "Yep. Meet my wife, Mackenzie."

Amusement played over Jacob's eyes. Kate still stared in wide-eyed shock. And, was that...hurt there too? Helen stood to the side, rolling her lips and eyeing her two sons. For too long, no one moved. Spoke. Breathed?

"Yes, sir." Conner, the military boy, finally severed the weird stillness. He stood, sauntered behind Jackson and Mackenzie, and squeezed their shoulders. "Shocked everyone. Can you believe it? Our funny man got married, and he didn't even invite us to the wedding. Poor Mom."

Helen laughed. It sounded nervous, but she grabbed on to Conner's lifeline. "Ah well. He did bring her home, so that counts for something. And think of all the trouble and expense they saved by eloping. Nothing wrong with that, I say." She stepped forward, patted Jackson's cheek and then touched Jacob's arm. "Why don't you and Kate get your things settled. I'll heat up some leftovers."

"No need, Mom." Jacob barely glanced at Helen. "Kate and I stopped at a restaurant on the way."

"Of course."

That was definitely an injured undertone in Helen's voice. No wonder. She'd spent half the day preparing a meal for her men. Jacob couldn't have called to let her know they weren't going to make it for dinner? Mackenzie ran another glance over both Jacob and Kate. Was Snobby one of the Seven Dwarfs? If so, Jacob was him. The pair stuck out as misfits in this rowdy, unrefined bunch even more than Mackenzie did.

Way more than Jackson did.

There was something there, lodged between Jackson, Jacob, and Kate. The duress was palpable, and inexplicably Mackenzie felt a defensiveness for the man currently holding her under his arm. Jackson's reasons for wanting her there were becoming clear, and though maybe a little pathetic—she'd probably be irritated with him when she had a chance to think it through—she immediately picked his side.

Sick in love? She could do that.

Shifting her weight, she leaned into him as if snuggling was all she ever wanted to do with this man. She laid her palm against his T-shirt, noticing the throb of his elevated heart rate.

"Mackenzie, was it?" Kate finally moved, apparently recovering from the stun Jackson had delivered.

"Yes." She smiled. Hopefully, it looked sweet. She didn't feel sweet toward this woman.

"I'm Kate. Jacob's wife." A delicate, well-manicured hand reached forward. "It's nice to meet you."

Mackenzie lifted her hand from the beat of Jackson's heart and met Kate's offer. "You too."

Kate held the greeting, but her eyes drifted toward Jackson again. Mackenzie felt sure her husband had met the woman's gaze. Felt the charge of whatever lay between them fire in the space, before Kate spoke again.

"Congratulations, Jackson."

"Thanks." His tone was nothing but easygoing. Something Mackenzie wondered if he'd mastered as a deflection.

"You're happy?" Kate asked.

And how was that for rude? His wife was standing right there.

"Very." Nothing in Jackson's voice hinted that he lied.

Chapter Six
(in which Jackson and Mackenzie hike to the ridge)

"You could have told me." Mackenzie trekked up the path, the clean scent of morning, earth, and pine filling her senses.

As if he didn't hear her, Jackson pushed his long strides up the ridgeline trail. After a family breakfast and a morning much more subdued than the previous day's, he'd announced they were going to hike the bluff. Just the two of them.

Mackenzie's first thought had been a snarky *Thanks for asking.* She bit her tongue before the words came out and sent him a tight smile.

"You always did love that view," Kate had said from her prim place on a wingback chair. Still in her pink silk pajamas, her hair brushed to perfection, lips a glossy rose, and sipping her tea as if she were born to nobility, she landed her attention on Jackson. Only Jackson.

He didn't answer. Instead, he buried his hand in Mackenzie's thick, wild, mophead hair and gave her neck a gentle squeeze. They'd gone back to the dungeon minutes later, where Mackenzie voiced her real thoughts.

"Thanks for the heads-up on this," she said.

"Do you want to stay here all day and watch the prince and princess turn the castle to ice?"

She frowned, studying him, wanting to dig in to the obviously convoluted backstory. But the basement wasn't exactly private, and Jackson had been one giant, knotted muscle cramp since Jacob and Kate had arrived the night before. When he'd hauled her up against him last night as she'd shivered in his sweatshirt yet again, he didn't relax. Not like the night before. She doubted he'd slept at all.

Instead of digging in to the past right there in the basement, Mackenzie sorted through the practicalities. "I don't have shoes for hiking. And I only brought my wool dress coat."

Jackson looked her over, his inspection nothing of interest other than to gather practical information. "You and Mom are about the same build. I'll see if she's got something you can borrow."

"Isn't there something else we could do?" Hiking wasn't an activity she was familiar with. Surely they could drive down to town. Get a latte.

A deep frown carved his face. It looked wrong on this man who was usually only smiles—even if those grins were often sharp and sarcastic.

"I need to breathe," he said. "But if you don't want to come, that's fine. I'm sure you'll find something to entertain yourself with here. Or you can take the car to town."

A whole morning and afternoon to herself? After forty-eight hours in this jam-packed house, that sounded delightful. She wasn't used to being constantly around people. She'd craved time alone. And yet the thought of him storming through the woods by himself, steeping in whatever was going on, made her edgy. He'd wanted her to go with him, and turning him down didn't seem right.

I'm not actually his wife, argued the selfish part of her. Quickly following that sassy thought was *Um, yes, actually, you are. For the moment.*

Not that she knew how to be a wife or had ever had the inclination to try it.

Still, she'd nodded, he'd found her some shoes, loaned her a long-sleeved shirt that she'd put on under his sweatshirt, and they set off.

She'd waited until they were securely out of earshot before she'd spoken. Jackson continued his march.

"Jackson." She snagged his arm, pulled him to a halt.

He spun, towering over her in a way that felt a little intimidating. "Could have told you what?"

So he had heard. "That you're in love with your brother's wife. You could have just told me that's why I'm here."

Jackson snorted, rolled his shoulders back, and looked toward the sky. "Here we go."

"Excuse me?"

Hands bracing his hips, he looked back at her. "Jacob and Kate have nothing to do with you and me. Get that out of your head."

"Really?"

He crossed his arms, leaned over her. "Really."

"So you think last night is normal? You think the fire between you and Kate is normal?"

His mouth flattened.

"There's nothing normal about dragging a woman you barely know to your family's get-together, playing like you're in love with her, and shoving it in a brother's face whom you clearly do *not* like."

"Nothing about anything between you and me is normal, Kenz. I'm not sure you have a point."

She stepped forward, tipping her head to keep their smoldering eye contact. "Why am I here?"

"Because I want you to be here."

"Why?"

His fiery look simmered. Gaze shifted, traveled over her face, and a flicker of tenderness softened the frown that had hardened his mouth.

"Jackson?" She hadn't meant for that to be breathy.

He reached to tuck a loose wave of her auburn hair back

into the messy bun she'd thrown together. The move was slow, unsure, and sent a shiver over her neck and arms.

"I don't know," he said, voice low. After another breath, he stepped back, opening space between them that she hadn't realized had vanished.

What was this pull between them? She shouldn't care what he thought or how he felt. Three days ago, she hadn't cared. She'd loathed his cocky swagger, his easy sarcasm, his infuriating stubbornness. And he'd blackmailed her into this sham. But when he looked to the ground, then began to turn away, she reached for his hand.

"Jackson."

Those long, warm fingers curved around hers, and he looked back at her.

"You have no reason to keep secrets from me. I'm nobody. Nothing to you."

The space between his eyebrows pinched, as if something hit him painfully. "What?"

"You can tell me what happened. There's nothing here for you to lose. I'll play the game. Be the doting, lovesick wife while we're here. You have my word."

He turned back to her, the study of his gaze intense and a little wild. Thoughts turned in his head, she was certain. What they were, she couldn't guess. If she were to try, she'd say they were memories. Hard ones.

"I'm not in love with Kate." His hand slipped from hers. "I haven't been for a while. Not sure I ever really was. Infatuated, yes. But I don't think it was love."

She missed his hand, and after his look made a slow, savory trail over her face again and then slipped to the earth at their feet, she missed that too.

"What happened?"

Shoving his hands into his pockets, Jackson shrugged. "She was a new girl at school our senior year. Pretty, and so far above me, I got neck cramps from tipping back to gawk at her. I couldn't believe she said yes when I asked her out. We dated. I thought it was going somewhere—did everything I could think of to impress her." He paused, peeked at her with a raised eyebrow. "For the record, she's high maintenance. Turned out Kate had a thing for my good-looking, going-places-fast big brother. I was just a rung on her ladder."

"And you resent her for it."

"No." The word was definitive, and he lifted his chin to meet her eyes again, as if to be sure she believed him. "I did. But it's been six years, Kenz. Six years of me getting on with my life. Six years of this extended...I don't know what. Just weirdness. Jacob has always been...superior. And that's fine. He can have his high-rise life—I've never wanted it. But with Kate, it's like she's the barb he likes to rub in. The silent gloat that says *you'll always be Dopey*. And she's...well, ridiculous. Did you see the way she looks at me? Talks to me? Like I'm pathetic. Like I'm the stray dog at the pound no one wants."

"Yeah, I saw."

"I can't stand it."

He turned, facing the gap of trees that overlooked the back side of the Murphys' property. A mist settled in the valley beyond the house, the white a crisp contrast to the deep green of the rolling hills and forests. The view was beautiful; Mackenzie could see why he loved it. If he did. Maybe that had been Kate being weird with him though. Pretending like she knew him so well, like she cared.

Mackenzie stepped closer, and he glanced down at her.

"I have a life, Kenz. A good life. A life I like. So don't feel sorry for me. *For the love of cats*, please don't be standing there drowning in pity for me. That'd be so much worse than Kate's crap."

She chuckled. "Okay."

Stillness settled between them, allowing the rustling of the evergreens and the movement of birds to fill the silence. Mackenzie looked up at the man beside her. Jackson stared at the valley, his look distant and unreadable. She lifted her hand, brushed his fingers with hers. His fingertips wiggled, feathering against her knuckles, wrist, and palm before taking hold of her hand. With the turn of his neck, the lowering of his chin, his attention zeroed in on her again.

"Swear you won't."

"Won't..." she puzzled. "Won't tell?"

"Won't feel sorry for me."

"Oh." Her face relaxed. "Okay. I swear it. I most definitely don't feel sorry for you, Jackson Murphy. You're too much of a pain in my neck to feel pity for."

The corners of his mouth lifted.

She mirrored his wispy smile. "Also, for future reference, I don't actually love cats."

It took a minute, his look confused for a breath. Then he laughed, the full smile much more the Jackson Murphy she knew.

Well, the bit of him she knew. She had a feeling that bit was more than most of his family knew. But she'd not feel sorry for him.

She might feel something though.

***

Mackenzie wasn't what he'd expected. She was so much better than he'd hoped. How had he mixed her up in his mind as being just another Kate Write Murphy—a demanding pain in the butt extraordinaire?

Kenz was absolutely nothing like Kate. Thank you for that. The woman sitting at the top of the bluff to his right was stubborn, yes. And sometimes hoity-toity—and oh, how he loved getting a rise out of her. But she didn't mean to be snobby. She was fiercely independent. Didn't need him for vanity strokes, a lazy crutch, or his wallet. All reasons that, more and more, he liked the woman he was calling his wife.

Sitting there in the late-morning sun, with a light mist swirling around her, she was also quite stunning. Not in the runway, A-list-girl way Kate had been. But in a down-to-earth, unpretentious, and snag-his-breath sort of way.

Sunlight caught the copper of her hair, dancing with the

red highlights and brown lowlights. Sharp intelligence gleamed from her rich eyes as she examined the outstretched valley below. Mackenzie would never be the kind of woman who'd play dumb as if it were attractive. She met him wit for wit, and their verbal spars were more fun than he should probably admit.

Jackson found himself wondering what would have been had they met in other circumstances. A normal one where he was completely sober and not entirely impulsive. Where they didn't end up regretfully married after a reckless, stupid night about which he could only patch bits and pieces of memories together.

What if he'd met her on a street as they went about their real life? Their eyes would have connected as she passed by, because he would have noticed that mass of auburn hair and would have checked to see what kind of face went with it. He would have smiled, because she was pretty. Likely, she would have arched an eyebrow, and he would have taken that as a challenge. And oh, he did love a challenge. He would have asked her out for coffee. Maybe a late lunch. She would have turned him down flat.

And then?

He'd never know. That wasn't their story.

The Jackson and Mackenzie story was a sham, and it would end with a signed paper, sealed by the state, stating that everything between them had been an insane mistake. Annulled. Void. Declared invalid.

And life would go on.

The thought spiked pain into his chest. A deep, hollow ache that seemed out of place for what was real between them—which wasn't much. Perhaps the sharp stab came from the whole married thing—the fact that he had never, not once in his life, thought of marriage as something disposable. In his belief marriage was sacred. And even if he'd jumped into that sacred commitment drunk and stupidly reckless, he'd still done it. Had the video on his phone to prove it. Even if the state of Nevada and Mackenzie Thornton could declare that moment in his life void and irrelevant, he couldn't. Wouldn't.

But also, possibly there was ache because he liked the feel of her hand in his. He'd grown instantly fond of calling her *wife* and rather delighted in the name Mackenzie Murphy.

What if...

She turned from the eastern view, tipped her face to catch his eye, and his thoughts dissolved. A peace and a sense of team had sprung between them somewhere between her reluctant agreement to this hike and the summit.

"It is a good view," she said.

He took it as an invitation and stepped five feet between to lower onto the boulder at her side. "One of the best."

"So you do love it."

He glanced at her, not sure what she meant.

"Kate wasn't wrong," she said.

Oh. Somehow his prissy ex-girlfriend-turned-sister-in-law managed to follow him all the way up there. Not what he wanted. "How about we leave Kate out of our conversations from now on?"

"Why?"

"Because they were more fun before."

"Our conversations?"

"Right."

"That was banter. Not conversation."

His smiled widened. Kenz waited, but he held out. Her mouth twisted into a smirk, and she breathed a small laugh. "Okay. She is nothing between you and me."

Let it be forever so.

She turned back toward the view, her mouth still soft and slightly upturned. A small shiver ran over her jaw, and she bundled her hands into the sleeves of his sweatshirt, which swallowed her small body. He looked at the shoes he'd borrowed from his mom and shook his head.

"Let me ask you something," he said.

"Okay..."

"Have you ever actually been outside, on something other than a sidewalk, for longer than say, ten minutes?"

She turned to him with that look that said she thought he was bizarre. A look he kind of found adorable. "What?"

"How about to the mountains. Have you ever been up here before?"

"What on earth are you talking about?"

"I brought you to the mountains, and all you packed were heeled dress boots, a wool dress coat, and clothes that have no practical use but to cover your body."

"I thought that's what clothes were for." She tucked her arms closer to her chest.

"You're freezing."

"As you've pointed out, we're in the mountains. And it's December."

"You didn't pack a coat. Or shoes to walk in."

"Right. We've already established that."

"Do you own either?"

"Where are you going with this?"

Other than the fact that watching her shiver was provoking an urge to wrap her close and see what happened from there, Jackson wasn't sure. But quick thinking was in his line of work.

"My wife will need some Christmas gifts under the family tree from her new husband. It would look off otherwise. That's all. Want to tell me your size?"

"Is that rhetorical?"

He shrugged. "I'll find out either way."

"Oh." She fiddled with the cuff of his sweatshirt. "These boots are a little big. Maybe a seven would be better." Her lips rolled together, a tell he'd already figured on her. She was thinking.

"What about you?" she said. "What should I get you?"

"Nothing."

"But that won't look right. What if someone says—"

He covered her hands, both of them twisted within the sleeves of the sweatshirt. "I'll tell them you married me. That's all I wanted." He lifted her chin with his index finger. "Don't get me anything."

Her stare froze on him, and he held it. Puffs of white breath materialized and evaporated, and his focus shifted from her eyes to her mouth. Lips he knew to be soft. He'd like to know again. He leaned slowly, and thought she did too. But before the space between them vanished, she pulled away and scooted off the rock.

Chapter Seven
(in which Mackenzie spends the day with Helen)

"Jackson." Mom finished covering the overnight French toast bake she'd put together, sparing a smile for him as he wandered into the kitchen. She lifted the dish from the counter. "What are you doing up here?"

Jackson met her at the fridge and opened the door for her. The light within the appliance added to the dim under-counter lighting he'd installed for her last summer. Other than that, the kitchen, and the rest of the main floor, was dark. Dad sat at the island—obviously he and Mom had been talking. Everyone else had retreated to their rooms for the evening. Rather early for a Murphy gathering. Well, for most of them.

"Just came up to make some hot cocoa," he said.

"Oh." Mom grabbed his arm. "Is it too cold in that basement?"

"It's a little chilly. But don't worry about it. We're fine." He thought about the easy excuse he had to wrap an arm around Kenz on that dreadful hide-a-bed they were sharing. All the discomfort—and the aching back he'd acquired because of it—had been worth it. Which was a bit mysterious.

"Are you and Kenz... uh..." Mom paused, wiped her hands

on her half apron, and sighed.

"We're good, Mom."

"I'd hoped so." Her expression pulled inward, pained. "I was so worried about having her meet your brother." She paused. "And Kate."

"That stuff was a long time ago, Mom."

"I know. But she's..."

"Oh, let it go, Helen." Dad chuckled. "They'll figure it out."

Mom shot him a scowl. "I know that. It's just that Kate is..."

"Kate is Kate." Jackson reached to the stove top to grab the teapot. "And she'll always be Kate. Makes no difference to me. Or to Kenz."

"Does Kenz know..."

Mom really couldn't finish a sentence tonight, which meant she'd been stewing on this for a while. "Yes. She knows I dated Kate. It's fine. We're all fine, Mom. I promise."

Jackson finished filling the teapot from the tap and set it onto the stove. The ignitor ticked, and then the gas flame burst up, the blue-and-orange heat adding a new glow to the dim kitchen.

"I like her, Jackson," Mom said.

He laughed. "That's good. A relief."

"I wasn't sure about her, the first day. She seemed so overwhelmed by all of us."

"We're an overwhelming crew," Dad said. "Anyone would be stunned walking into this circus. Especially a woman who'd grown up as an only child."

Jackson leaned his backside against the counter and crossed his arms. "We are something else, for sure." He laughed quietly. "She was sure mortified when I told her about the first time Matt brought Lauren here."

Dad pinned a look on him and then shook his head. "You're lucky Matt didn't take you into the woods and make you dig your own grave."

"Yes, well," Mom said. "Mackenzie certainly showed some moxie when your brothers ambushed you yesterday morning."

Dad and Jackson both laughed.

"She did that," Dad said. "I like her all the more for it. She already had my approval, for the record. She's smart, and she doesn't take nonsense from you, Jack. I think she'll keep you on your toes and make your life interesting."

"Definitely true already." Guilt jabbed Jackson's conscience. He was standing there lying to his parents. Sort of.

What would they say, do, if he admitted what had really happened? Part of him almost wanted to—wanted to hear what they thought he should do about this Vegas marriage that Mackenzie was already in the process of dissolving. But the high probability that Mom would cry and Dad would scowl, and the fact that they'd be massively disappointed in him, far outweighed the part that wanted their counsel.

"Actually, Mom, I was wondering if you'd be willing to do something for me." Switching tracks, both mentally and in this conversation, was a much safer plan.

"Of course, son."

"I need to do some Christmas shopping, and Kenz can't come."

Dad snorted. "First Christmas together, and you're already scrambling for last-minute gifts?"

"Yeah. I learned from the king of last-minute gifts. Speaking of which, what'd you get Mom?"

Dad crossed his arms. "That's classified information."

"Right."

"You'll find out tomorrow when we go to town to get it," Dad added.

"Exactly."

Mom shook her head. "I'll warn Kenz to expect a lifetime of this. And she can hang out with Lauren and me tomorrow, if that's what you were asking."

"That'd be perfect, Mom. Thanks."

"We'll be working on some arrangements—doing a tutorial, and I'll need to take some shots of them, as well as some of my Christmas cookies for the blog. Will she mind, do you think?"

"I doubt it." Actually, Jackson couldn't say for sure one way or the other if Kenz would actually mind or not. Didn't know her well enough for that. But he was sure that she'd play along. She'd been a good sport like that so far.

Steam from the hot water made the whistle on the teapot chirp, and Jackson shut off the heat. Mom turned to the glass-front cabinet and pulled down two large mugs, both with holly painted on the front.

"Do you need more blankets down there?" Dad asked as Jackson pulled the canister of Mom's homemade hot cocoa mix from a cabinet.

Jackson was tempted to say no. But that would be entirely selfish. Kenz had been cold, and the fact that he liked the feel of her in his arms wasn't a good reason to keep her that way. "Yeah, maybe one more thick quilt would be good."

"You could have taken the other queen bed upstairs, you know." Dad lifted an eyebrow. "First come, first serve."

Filling the mugs, Jackson snorted. "Yeah. That would have gone over super well with Jacob."

"He knows how this works."

"I know how he works." Jackson stirred both mugs, tapped the spoon on the edge of the last one, and tossed it into the dishwasher. Jacob and Kate would have left. As much as Jackson hated the weirdness between them, he hated the way Jacob kept injuring their mother with his snobbery more. "Really, Dad, Kenz and I are fine. Hot cocoa and a blanket, and we're good."

***

Mackenzie woke up warm. The extra blanket had helped, but when Jackson had slung an arm around her again sometime in the night, she must have burrowed into him. Now his breath came soft and easy against her forehead, the restful rhythm telling her he was still asleep. Which meant she could stay right where she was.

She shut her eyes and indulged in a time of *let's pretend this is real.*

***

"Come on, lover boy." A pillow hit Jackson's head a moment after Connor's voice filtered through his sleepy haze. "Dad says you're shopping with us, so let's go."

Jackson grunted as the woman in his arms buried deeper into his chest. *My wife.* His heart stirred a little painfully, and he moved his arms to cocoon her head from another incoming blow.

"Get out of here, ape," he grumbled. "Don't you have any manners?"

"Only when an officer's around. Get up."

And there was that second blow to the head.

"All right." Jackson pushed up on his elbow and reached for the stupid pillow, snagging it on the upswing. "I'm up. Get out of here."

"Right." Connor tossed the pillow at him. "No goofing around either. I don't care if you're newlywed—I'll come back down here if you're not upstairs, dressed, and ready to go in five minutes."

The marching rhythm of Connor's feet on the stairs announced his departure, and Jackson looked down at the redhead in his bed. Eyes still closed, full mouth tipped in a small smile, and one hand tangled in that soft mass of hair, she looked exactly like what he wanted to wake up to every morning for the rest of his life.

What if...

"Your brother is demanding."

"Yes. I'd say courtesy of the military, but that would be a lie. He's always been a boss."

Her grin grew, and her eyes fluttered open and then squinted up at him. "You like him. He's the brother you're closest to."

He couldn't help staring at her. Nor could he resist fingering the lock of auburn that draped over her forehead. "You have that figured, do you?" What else did she have figured about him? Could she read what he was thinking right then?

Probably she did, because her smile faded, and she rolled away. "Better get going. Doubt Connor was joking about the five minutes."

"Probably not." He didn't move, watching her push off the bed, noticing, not for the first time, how small she looked in his sweatshirt. He wondered if it would smell like her when she was done with it, all spring-ish and warm. And speculated whether or not she realized that she'd rolled into him somewhere around midnight, as if she'd wanted him to hold her.

Mackenzie glanced at him while he tracked her progress across the room, and a blush crept up her neck. He'd been staring, and she'd caught him. Heaven help him, but that blush might be telling.

"Hope you're moving down there, Jackson!" Connor's military, no-nonsense holler wafted from the top of the stairs. "Ice bucket is next."

Jackson flung the covers off his legs. "I'm up."

Kenz disappeared around the corner, headed toward the bathroom. He followed, very aware that he might get a hissing earful for the presumption, but when he reached the door, it was still open, and he found her stretching in front of the shower.

"You'll be okay with my mom and Lauren?" He snatched his toothbrush.

"Sure."

Toothpaste in one hand, brush in the other, he looked at her. "Really?"

"I'm a big girl, Jackson. A day with your mom and sisters-in-law won't kill me."

"Well." He went back to applying toothpaste. "A day with

Lauren won't, anyway."

"Be nice."

"Always." He winked, shoved the toothbrush in his mouth, and got to work.

Kenz slid past him, reaching for her overnight bag. "Hurry up. I need a shower."

He spit into the sink. "Right. I'll need my sweatshirt." Small lie. He didn't need *that* sweatshirt. He had two others in his bag. But he wanted *that* sweatshirt.

With a shrug, she slipped the bulky thing over her head and continued to gather her soaps in her tank top.

Man, he was asking for trouble with this.

***

"Are you sure you don't mind, sweetie?" Helen touched Mackenzie's hand, which rested on the concrete counter in the Murphys' greenhouse.

"I think so."

"You really don't have to be in the video, if you'd prefer not." Lauren smiled warmly, her tone genuine. "Don't get me wrong—we'd love for you to be. It's just that Helen's blog is pretty popular, and her tutorials get a lot of hits. So you just need to know that up front."

Wishing she'd thought to look up *A Touch of Home* on her phone last night, Mackenzie nodded. "If you think your followers would like to see someone learning how it's done, I'm good with being that girl. Be forewarned though. I didn't grow up in a crafty kind of home, so I'll be completely ignorant."

That was putting it mildly. Mother steered clear of anything that might be conjured as *a woman's domain*. Flower crafts would most certainly fall into that. As would Christmas cookies.

A thread of curiosity pulled in her mind about all of it. Perhaps the intrigue of the unknown. She was truly interested in what Helen and Lauren had to show her, as much as she was inspired by the room Kevin had built specifically for his wife's hobby-turned-cyber-business.

The greenhouse, which was an add-on attachment to the main house, smelled of pine, eucalyptus, and a variety of more subtle floral scents. Large, white-paned windows spanned the walls on three sides of the twelve-by-twenty space, and beneath them, a narrow ledge held an assortment of live plants. Along the wall that used to be the exterior of the Murphy home sat a large, see-through refrigerator full of blossoms. A stone fireplace anchored the center of the southern wall, and the fire burning within its hold crackled and snapped.

On the west side, by a pair of heavy white French doors, a group of small potted evergreens sat on the heated tile floor. Mackenzie assumed they were Matt and Lauren's, from their infant Christmas tree farm—which Matt had hoped he and Lauren might find a niche market for, as they wanted to sell small, live, pre-decorated trees. Helen's established audience with *A Touch of Home* was the perfect foot in the door, Lauren had said.

"All right then." Hellen handed Mackenzie a folded white apron. "We'll get ourselves set up while Lauren gets the camera ready. You'll want the covering, because the stems will be wet, and some might have lingering sap. Also, are you allergic to anything?"

"Not that I know of."

"Perfect." Helen ducked into her apron and wrapped the strings with the ease of practice.

Mackenzie slipped her apron on as well and watched Helen pull items from the shelving below the long island, taking note as Jackson's mother named her material.

"We've got our containers—a few different types, for varied shapes and sizes. And floral foam. Trust me—floral foam is our friend."

Lauren snickered. "If you don't mind the crumbly, gritty stuff getting in your fingernails."

Helen shot her a friendly yet sassy smile. "I am still baffled how you can at once be such a green thumb and tactile defensive."

"I use gloves in the field." Lauren laughed. "And scrub my hands almost raw when we're done."

"I believe that, poor girl." Helen snagged Lauren's hand and lifted it for inspection. "Knuckles are so dry, they bleed."

The closeness and friendship between the two women pulled at Mackenzie. Was this normal?

Helen hefted a bucket of mixed flowers—Mackenzie recognized only the hydrangeas and roses—and Lauren followed her back to the island, hauling a second bucket, that one full of the evergreen boughs they'd cut the day before.

"All right, my sweet daughters." Helen pressed palms onto the concrete counter and smiled at Lauren and Mackenzie. "Are we ready to have some fun?"

"Let's do it." Lauren winked and slipped to the other side of the counter, where she'd set up the tripod for the camera.

While Mackenzie wondered if the isolated, chilled life she'd grown up with was odd or if this warm and open relationship between Helen and Lauren was the strange one, the other two women began. It didn't take long for Mackenzie to stop pondering which scenario was not normal, because Helen and Lauren drew her into their kindness within the first twenty minutes of their work.

"We'll start with this rustic box, turning it into a unique centerpiece for a large Christmas table. Before we get into the details, I want to introduce the newest Murphy addition." Helen turned her attention from Lauren and the camera to Mackenzie, her warm smile helping Mackenzie to relax. "This is my son Jackson's new bride, Mackenzie, and Lauren and I are thrilled to have her in the greenhouse with us today."

"Woo-hoo," Lauren said from behind the scene. "More estrogen to combat this Murphy house full of men."

Helen laughed and lifted her hands skyward. "My prayers are being answered."

"Amen."

Mackenzie grinned at their banter.

"What do you think, Kenz?" Helen asked. "Did you ever imagine you'd marry into a family of seven boys?"

"Not once."

"It's a little nuts, isn't it?" Lauren asked, again off screen.

Mackenzie shrugged. "Definitely louder than what I was used to. But I was an only child. It was just my mother and me."

"Well, I certainly hope my rowdy bunch doesn't scare you off."

Mackenzie smiled, not sure what she could say that wouldn't be an outright lie or an exposure of the truth.

What was going to happen after this week? When she and Jackson filed that petition for annulment and their lives unwound? Had he thought about that? About what he'd tell this lovely woman beside her?

Mackenzie's heart throbbed as she imagined him telling Helen. At the way Helen's smile would slip, the way she'd be both hurt and disappointed in her son. And in Mackenzie. For some reason, that mattered.

"Okay, we're going to get started on our demonstrations for today. As always, if you're a local viewer, I do take special orders and have a few flowers left for some last-minute arrangements. Also, we'll have my other sweet daughter-in-law on in the next frame, and we'll be decorating one of her live mini-Christmas trees. Stick around."

With that, Helen got started, her demonstration hands on as she showed Mackenzie how to put together a rustic, full, beautiful centerpiece using the various evergreen boughs, white hydrangeas, and red berries. Somewhere in between soaking the floral foam, lining the box with poly foil, and designing the arrangement, Mackenzie lost herself.

The muscles in her neck and shoulders unwound, making her aware that they'd been tight for quite a while. Since the day she'd gotten married. Maybe even longer.

They arranged several more pieces, shot more video footage. Lauren showed Mackenzie how to wrap the live mini-trees in the poly foil, and Mackenzie decorated a two-foot-tall fir alongside her sister-in-law. Then, while Lauren edited and spliced video, Mackenzie helped Helen put most of the creations in the refrigerator—each one of them already sold on preorder from someone in town. They wiped down the concrete work surface, pulled out cookies from the kitchen refrigerator, and arranged them for a photo shoot with a few of the newly created centerpieces.

"And that's a wrap!" Helen clapped her hands after she snapped the last picture. "I'll upload all of this tonight, and it'll be live for Christmas Eve."

"Bet it'll be your most popular post yet," Lauren said.

Mackenzie definitely would be checking out *A Touch of Home*. Likely, more than once, and long after she and Jackson went their separate ways. Hopefully, watching the videos, and seeing whatever else Helen and Lauren posted, would allow the feeling of this day to linger as she stepped back into her normal life.

She wasn't sure what to call that feeling. But she wished it was something she could keep.

Chapter Eight

(in which Mackenzie experiences a Murphy Christmas)

"We've got a few minutes, and I need to say some things to you." Connor leaned on the small table between them at the Storm Café.

Jackson froze, hand on his coffee mug, and forced himself to look at his brother.

"That video you texted me..." An eyebrow arched. "Level with me, little brother."

Swallowing, Jackson glanced across the little restaurant—a local treasure he visited every time he came home and missed when he was gone. Dad continued to visit with Harrison at the diner counter, a man from the church the Murphys had attended forever.

"What about it?"

"I know drunk when I see it." Connor's mouth drew flat.

Why on earth had Jackson texted anything to anyone about that weekend in Vegas? Then again, why had he done most of anything that he'd done that Saturday night? At least it'd only been Connor. Connor kept his nose clean and his mouth shut.

Except, why was he bringing it up?

Jackson looked at the mug still in his hand. "I don't drink that much. Usually." Especially not lately. Meeting Sean had helped him iron out some things in his life, and he'd been walking in a good direction. Something he'd wished his family would acknowledge, even just a little bit.

"You were drunk," Connor said flatly.

But there was that. Pulse throbbing, Jackson nodded.

"And so was Mackenzie."

Another slow dip of his head.

"And this marriage?"

What did Connor want him to say?

His brother leaned closer. "Had you even known each other before that weekend?"

"No." The answer came out tight and low.

"Yet you brought her home to meet Mom and Dad."

Jackson eyed his brother, shame quickly morphing into irritation. "You said Mom wanted to meet her. What do you want from me?"

"Just want to know how far you've thought this through. You brought a girl home as your wife. That's kind of a game changer, you know?"

Pinning his lips together, Jackson rolled his free hand into a fist.

Connor continued to press. "How long you think this is going to last?"

Anger gave way to defeat, and Jackson felt it press on his shoulders like granite. A long sigh rattled from his chest. "Look, this stays between you and me. For now. Got it?"

"Haven't said anything to anyone yet."

Jackson waited, piercing his brother with a look that felt both threatening and desperate. "Kenz already has the paperwork done. For an annulment. I told her I wasn't signing them unless she came up here with me for the week."

"Why?"

Jackpot question. There were several reasons, but they all seemed sketchy. Except one.

"I married her, Connor." He held a firm look. "Doesn't seem right to say it was a mistake and move on. It just doesn't feel right."

Connor's shoulders rolled forward. "Lots of people make mistakes and move on. Do you really think lying about it all is going to work out?"

"I'm not lying—I just told you. I *married* her. Legally, she's my wife."

"But pretending that it's love?"

"What if it could be?" His answer came out in a rush before he really thought about it. But yeah, what if? "What if it could work out?"

Connor watched him, questions in his eyes.

"I like her. More every day."

"I can see that. And I'll admit to you that she's a much better fit for you than Kate was. But marriage? It's supposed to start with love."

"Because that always works out. What's the divorce rate in this country again?" Jackson pushed back from the table and leaned against the chair. "What if it started with commitment? With me saying that I'm not willing to trash it because of the stupid way I'd jumped into it?"

"So that's what's happening? Because you just told me Kenz—"

Jackson cleared his throat and shot Connor a warning glare. Dad was shaking hands with Harrison, signaling an end to his conversation. Connor's lips closed for a moment, and then he lifted his mug, shielding his mouth from one side.

"I'm worried for you, Jackson. That's all. Think you're making a bad situation worse, and now you've got Mom and Dad mixed up in it. But I've got your back."

"Thanks." Sort of.

Dad turned, strode back to their table, and Jackson said something about Sunday night football. Safe conversation about things that didn't have real meaning. They finished their lunch, hit a few more stores, where Jackson found a black winter coat and a pair of warm winter boots for his wife, picked out a watch for his mom, had them all gift wrapped, and then made their way back up the hill toward home.

Where he could continue playing happily ever after with Kenz. As long as Connor kept his word. Good thing Kenz had been right—of all his brothers, Jackson was closest to Connor.

Still, the charade felt more dangerous. Perhaps because of the things he'd confessed out loud to his brother. True things. Things he needed to find a way to tell Kenz before his time was up.

He liked her. More, he'd married her. That mattered, even if no one else understood, and he had a deep desire to make it work. Which was a problem, because she wasn't on the same page.

***

Mackenzie had known Christmas as "winter holiday." As a time for her to load up on books that didn't require high levels of concentration. A time to eat a little bit of junk usually forbidden in their home. And on the actual holiday, she and Mother would exchange a few high-dollar, though fairly meaningless, gifts, travel to her grandparents' home in San Diego, dine in their opulent home overlooking the beach, only to travel back that same night so as to avoid any meaningful discussions. A.k.a. arguments.

The rest of winter holiday was spent on her own. Just Mackenzie and the secret friends she made in books. The first time she'd sneaked *Little House on the Prairie* home, she'd felt a rush of guilt threading with a strange sense of freedom. Mother's reading list for her had been extensive—and often she'd preach about how she'd allow her daughter to read what many parents had banned for theirs, because of "radical free thinking that has been repeatedly doused by our patriarchal society." As a young girl, Mackenzie had hardly understood what that meant. What she did understand was that the yellow book with the wagon on the cover would not meet with Mother's approval. Mackenzie had yet to grip why.

Mother was an enigma. A strong force Mackenzie hadn't ever fought against and had given up understanding.

That year, at the end of Christmas day, the one spent with Jackson's family in all of its loud, crowded, togetherness, Mackenzie wondered how Mother would have responded to this very *other* holiday. No, she knew how Mother would have responded. Silent as an owl perched in a corner, overlooking the chaos with disdain, she would have said absolutely nothing. Spoken to no one. Later, when it was just Mackenzie in her presence, she'd shame the Murphys for everything from their massive carbon footprint to the fact that Helen was the exemplified reason women *still* didn't own the respect they should be demanding.

Strange that. The men in this home generally adored Helen Murphy. And by all appearances, Jackson's mother was genuinely happy.

The day, though a bit overwhelming because everything was so foreign, settled into Mackenzie's heart as something soft and lovely. As she slipped beneath the pile of blankets onto that crunchy mattress that was becoming more laughable than horrendous with every passing night, Mackenzie stored up the memories with cherished care. The cinnamon rolls and hot cocoa for breakfast. The loud chaos, filled with laughter as presents were distributed and opened. The quiet, settled feeling, upheld by a sense of communal joy while Kevin Murphy read the story of Jesus's birth straight from a black leather-bound Bible. And the eating that lasted the rest of the day.

All the while, there had been Jackson. Ever at her side, playing the doting new husband. Grinning while she tried on the new coat and boots—and was she to return them to him when they went back to their separate lives? His arm slung around her neck, kiss pressed to her temple in response to Kate's rather pointed observation that he didn't have a gift from his wife.

"She married me," he had said, as promised. "That's everything."

In that moment, she wanted Mother to meet the man she'd married. Not because Mother would approve—she most certainly would not. But because Jackson Murphy was a man worthy of meeting.

That's everything. An odd response, especially from a fake-but-not-fake husband. One that warmed her heart even though it shouldn't. Words that stayed at the front of her mind long after she should have swept them clear.

"Cold?" Jackson asked from his side of their bed.

Lying on her back, she settled the blankets over her and turned her head to find his face in the dim light of his phone-turned-night-lamp. He had a handsome face. Dark eyes that often laughed. A groomed shadow beard that gave definition to his jawline. And lips that smiled as a default, made unique by the scar from what she assumed had been a cleft lip.

Her first impression of him hadn't diminished—Jackson Murphy was eye candy. But also, he wasn't the total jerk she'd thought him.

Mackenzie Thornton, however, wasn't *wife* material. Even if knowing this man a little better made him all the more attractive. They were from different worlds. Expected different things—and had different expectations placed upon them. This charade was exactly that—a pretense that was about to end.

She'd best keep that in the front of her mind, not those sweet words that continued to stir a longing within her.

"We go home tomorrow," she said.

She felt, more than saw, his study. Heard in the silence a hesitation that she couldn't understand. And yet felt in her own heart.

Several breaths passed between them, and then the small amount of light snuffed out. Still several more moments of strain and pull and feelings that she shouldn't feel. Then she rolled onto her side toward him, until she found the bulge of his shoulder.

"Yes," she whispered. "I'm cold."

The muscles in his arm tensed, and then he shifted too.

One more night. She'd sleep in his arms this one last time. And then it would all be over.

She'd return him where he belonged—just like those books she'd sneaked over her lonely winter holidays. Jackson would be filed into memory with those secret friends she wasn't allowed to have.

But she'd have these moments with him to revisit in the

security of her mind. Perhaps on the next winter holiday, when she was bound to feel loneliness more keenly than ever before.

She shut her eyes, willing sleep to come. A single, silent tear leaked onto her nose. She let it roll untouched.

Chapter Nine

(in which Mackenzie and Jackson go their separate ways)

Jackson tried to keep the two-hour drive back on the light side. Forced conversation about more details of their lives normal married people would already know. For a while, Kenzie played along, answering his questions with a tight smile.

An hour and a half into the trip, he asked, "Did you always want to be a doctor?"

That fake smile she'd worked so hard to keep faltered. Even with his focus mostly on the road, he could feel her steel.

"Kenz?"

"It's what I've always worked for," she said, voice clipped.

He glanced at her. Features that had gone soft somewhere around day two of their little married-couple facade had become hard again. Cold and distant—the way she'd looked when she'd shown up at the café with legal papers two weeks back. Pretty, but not the woman he'd just spent Christmas with.

The change was severe and almost painful to take in.

"Do you want to be a doctor?"

Her jaw clenched, and she shot him a warning look. "Doesn't matter."

"Why doesn't it matter?"

"I can't get into medical school, so what I want is irrelevant."

"But—"

"Jackson, quit. I don't want to talk about this. All of this getting-to-know-you-better stuff isn't necessary, and I don't want to talk anymore, okay?"

And just like that, she cut him off. Shoved him into a box, strapped it closed with packing tape, and labeled it *Return to Sender*. As if she wasn't interested at all. If he hadn't spent the past few days seeing a different version of her, he would have believed Kenz to be frigid and stiff and not worth the effort.

But she'd cried last night in his arms. He'd felt the tear soak into his cotton shirt. He'd wanted to cup her face in his hands, kiss the hurt away, and tell her they could figure this out.

That was assuming that tear had to do with him. Them. Pretty big assumption. He hadn't been brave enough to ask about it or to act. So he'd stayed silent, held her in the darkness, and prayed that he'd find courage and words somewhere between the basement of his parents' home and Mackenzie's front door.

The distance between last night and goodbye narrowed too quickly, and as the miles slipped by, the silence pushed against him.

By the time he pulled up to her townhouse, the space between them might as well have been the Pacific. Kenz let herself out of the vehicle while he lifted her bag from the back. She reached for the handle, but he held it away.

"I'll take it in for you," he said.

She studied him, her mouth pressed and a scowl wrinkling her forehead, and then nodded. The porchlight flicked on when they stepped into the range of the motion detector, and Kenz rattled the key into the lock. When the door finally surrendered, she stepped inside, took two strides, and then stopped to turn to him.

"Just leave it there." She pointed to her luggage. "I'll get it."

"You sure?"

"Of course." She unzipped the winter coat he'd given her and slipped it from her arms. "Here."

"What?"

"The boots are in the shopping bag in the backseat of your

truck." She pushed the coat toward him.

Jackson set the bag on the tiled floor, then gently guided the coat back to her chest. "It was a gift, Kenz. I'd rather you keep it."

Her gaze stayed on his face, a look of what he thought was distrust swimming in there. He slid nearer, longing to bring back the closeness he'd felt with her the past couple of days, begging God for the right words.

"You're making this really hard, Jackson." Tears sheened her eyes.

He shook his head. "What if—"

"Please don't." She stepped back, prying open the distance again. "We had a deal. I held up my end, did what you asked. Now we're done."

His heart thundered with panic, and he gripped her shoulder. "What if we're not?"

Silence throbbed, and Jackson lost himself in the electric connection between them. Was there hope there? The wish that he felt staring back at him? Pulling her hand to his chest, he leaned. "Please, Kenz..."

She laughed. It sounded sad, wistful, longing, and defeated all at once. "We can't, Jackson. Please accept that." Her fingers slid over his, and slowly, gently, she pried open his grip. "I never intended to get married. I don't mean that I never intended to marry *you*. I mean I never intended to marry at all. It's not a life for me."

"Why?"

"I..." Her brow furrowed, and she looked to the side. "I'm just not a wife kind of girl."

"What does that mean? What is a wife kind of girl?"

Her shoulders sagged as a sigh whispered from her. "It means that you and I are done. I'll admit that this week went better than I ever could have imagined. But it wasn't real, remember? I went because you asked me to—because you blackmailed me. And because that night in Vegas was my mistake too." She lifted her face back to him, resolve firm in her gaze. All traces of yearning gone. "That's all I owe you, Jackson. Now you owe me a signature."

His mind screamed against it. But he had promised her. *I also promised till death do us part.* At least, he thought that had probably been in his vows. Usually were. The memory on those details were sketchy though.

Who could build a life on such a monumental mistake? It was time to end it, to move on. Even if that wasn't what he wanted.

He closed a hand over the coat she'd extended to him again, took it, and laid it over the bag near their feet. With one step, he narrowed the gap between them and leaned to brush a kiss over her forehead.

"I'll mail the papers to you on Monday," he whispered.

Her hand cupped his shoulder, then slid down to his elbow, provoking that painful yearning in his chest. This was wrong. He knew it. Every cell within him protested.

"Goodbye, Jackson." She stepped back, taking with her the warm scent of orange blossoms and the stirring of her breath near his chest. And the slimmest possibility that they could be something more than one night in Vegas gone wrong.

"Keep the coat, Kenz." Against the strong objection of his heart, he let her go.

***

Her house felt empty. Too quiet. Alone had never felt like this—like everything had gone gray and color would never return.

Mackenzie pressed both palms against her bed. The plush mattress gave without a single crackling protest. She missed the sound of crunching plastic.

"Stop," she demanded, not allowing the building tears a release. Alyssa and Carmen weren't back yet, so she could talk to herself in this stark-lonely room. No one was there to think less of her for it. She pushed off the bed and returned to her bag, slowly unpacking, hanging up sweaters—half of which she hadn't worn because she'd slipped on Jackson's sweatshirt as often as possible. Such a flighty-girl-in-love thing to do.

It was like she'd become a different person up there with him.

No. That wasn't right. Couldn't be. Because she'd felt comfortable with herself in the Murphy home. Maybe for the first time in her life.

That made no sense either. She groaned, finished putting away her clothes, and moved to take her bag down to the storage room. When she came back upstairs, the only trace of her weeklong trip with Jackson was the black ski coat sitting on the floor of the entry. She snatched it up, moved to hang it in the entry closet, and then stopped.

No one was there to know the difference.

The coat went with her to her room. After changing into her gym shorts and tank top, she sank into that plush mattress with the coat in hand. It wasn't the same as Jackson's arm around her, his warm body nearby, but she buried her face into the fabric, shut her eyes, and let herself imagine that it was.

She didn't sleep well. The following morning, she didn't feel well either.

Sick enough, in fact, that she called into the lab at the hospital to let them know she wouldn't make it in. Hopefully it was just the twenty-four-hour stomach bug. She had a life to get on with.

Chapter Ten

(in which Mackenzie shows up on Jackson's front porch)

The new year had rolled by. Jackson had done what he'd promised—signed the petition for an annulment—and was expecting some kind of official something to tell him that Jackson and Mackenzie Murphy were never actually Jackson and Mackenzie Murphy. As if that one night had never happened.

What if every mistake made could be rendered invalid? Every error deleted? He fingered the scar on his upper lip, the one that had marked him as different from the other Murphy boys. The one that had, for so very long, silently whispered that he was a blotch.

That was a slippery slope, wasn't it?

The smell of pepperonis, cheese, tomato-basil sauce, and bread wafted throughout his kitchen. The fridge had been stocked, pizzas ready and waiting. But Jackson's mind wasn't anywhere near his plans for that Friday night.

Instead, as the thoughts about his marriage and about his cleft lip collided, a childhood memory took center stage. It had been a day of tears for his six-year-old self. A day that the other boys at school had been merciless, and his older brothers hadn't been much better. Mom had hugged him, set a glass of chocolate milk on the coffee table in front of him, and clicked on the TV—

something that stood out because it was not typical. With a few quick flicks of a button, a man with giant hair and a paint brush came onto the screen.

"Bob Ross," Mom had said, nodding to the guy talking and painting.

Jackson had sniffed. "I've seen him. You watch him sometimes."

"Right."

They watched together for a while.

"Mom?"

"Yes?"

"You don't paint."

"That's true. I like Mr. Ross though."

"Why?"

"I like how he teaches."

"But you still don't paint."

"No. But Mr. Ross, he teaches about life when he paints."

"Like my Sunday school teacher and her flannel graph?"

Mom laughed. "Well, no. Not quite like that. I don't know that he even means to teach about life. But watch."

So they watched some more. And then...

Mr. Ross made a mistake. Except, he chuckled. "Remember," the man said, smiling, using the brush on the blotch he'd just made. "There are no mistakes. Just happy accidents."

Jackson had been mesmerized as the man with the big hair transformed that blotch into part of the picture. It fit perfectly. As if it was exactly as he had intended in the first place.

The television flicked off.

"Jackson," Mom had said, hand on his head. "There are a lot of things in this world that are messed up. I would not have chosen for you to have a cleft lip, if I could have picked. But the thing is, son, God is even more talented, more powerful, than Mr. Ross is with his paints and brushes. When we have these messes, these mistakes, we can turn them over to God. In His hands they become a beautiful part of the whole picture." She ran a gentle finger down the scar that connected his nose, over his lip, and to his gum. "We're just going to have to trust Him to do it."

Jackson blinked at the memory that was, though distant, still so fresh it summoned deep emotion. With his thumb, he brushed that scar again, then leaned both palms against the counter, thinking again about what Sean had said about messes and messages.

I really wanted you to Bob Ross that night in Vegas.

Mackenzie, their marriage. Hadn't left his thoughts since he'd walked away three weeks before. Even now, that Friday night when he was expecting Connor and a couple of other buddies over for a night of *Company of Heroes*, he couldn't get her out of his mind. Their failed-from-the-start marriage off his heart.

He barely was able to push back the gloom enough to answer the door with a smile.

Connor, Sean, and two other guys filed into his little eight-hundred-square-foot two-bedroom house. Pulling on his experience as a part-time stand-up comedian, Jackson smiled, laughed. Told a few funny stories he had worked out in the deathly quiet hours that had felt suffocating over the past few weeks, and ate.

A few hours into *Heroes*, and he almost couldn't feel the ever-present throb of disappointment. So when the doorbell rang, he tossed his wireless control to the couch and meandered across the room to answer. He'd expected...well, he didn't know what he expected. A delivery from Amazon? Another pizza that Connor had ordered without telling him? Any number of possibilities...

Not her.

But there she was, standing off to the side, out of direct sight and on the edge of the halo light. Jackson's heart stalled, throat swelled, and breathing became foreign.

She looked up at him, her mouth unsmiling.

Head foggy, he swallowed. Scrambled to guess why she was there. Slowly, he stepped out of the house, pulling the door shut behind him. "Kenz." Her name felt like an ache on his breath. A prayer he'd been too raw to pray.

She looked...well, horrible. But beautiful. He doubted that it was possible for her to not be beautiful. Even with her hair piled helter-skelter atop her head, dressed in clothes that seemed baggy, and her face drawn as if she'd been sick, she was beautiful. But also, not well.

The numbness lifted, and he stepped forward again, hand reaching for her shoulder. "It's good to see you, Kenz."

She looked toward her feet and sniffed.

"Are you..." Alarm zipped through him, and he took another step nearer. "What's going on?"

Her shoulders quaked, and both hands covered her face. "I don't know what to do."

Something happened with the annulment. It'd been rejected. Would the state reject it? If so, that meant...

She looked up at him, the yellow light from overhead catching the sheen of her tears.

"It's okay." He lifted a hand, smudged the wet trail on her face with his thumb. "We'll fix it, okay?"

Divorce. He'd be divorced. Somehow that pierced deeper. Hadn't even been given a chance to work on his marriage. Just married and then divorced. Nothing but a short Christmas in between.

Her tears doubled, soft cries now sobs. He swallowed the bitterness. "Kenz, whatever I need to sign or do, just...it's okay. Tell me. I'll do it. We'll fix—"

"I'm pregnant."

Everything froze. The cold breeze from the distant coast stirring the trees, the ruckus happening in his living room, the low rumble of traffic on the freeway five blocks over. They all ceased to exist. Jackson knew nothing but the slow boom of his heart filling his ears as he stared down at her. The need for oxygen forced him to draw a breath, the expansion of his lungs painful against the ballooning panic.

Mackenzie's gut-deep cries quieted, though her lips still quivered. She watched him, wild fear in her eyes.

"You're..." Jackson swallowed again, desperately trying to assemble coherent thoughts. Make sensible words cross his lips.

"You're sure?"

"That I'm pregnant? Or that the baby is yours?"

He drew back, as if a knife had just plunged into his chest. "What?"

She shuffled through her purse, pulled out a ziplock bag, and shoved it against his chest, anger hot in her gaze. "I wouldn't be here if I didn't know."

Still trying to make his mind work, he took the baggie and held it up. Three thermometer-ish sticks met his inspection, every one of them with a pink plus in the view window.

One night, God! It was one night!

A baby. She was carrying his baby. He'd never even thought about...

Mackenzie slunk away, burying herself farther in the shadows before Jackson shook himself out of shock.

"Kenz, I didn't mean..."

She froze, arms wrapped around her body, as if she were shielding herself from an expected blow.

What do I do? This woman hadn't wanted him. Hadn't even wanted to try with him. Said they had no future together. But a baby?

Changed everything.

Jackson closed the space between them, cupped her face, and tipped it so that she'd look at him. "It's mine, and I know that. I'm just shocked."

A fresh trickle of tears leaked from her eyes, and a new, horrifying thought pressed into his mind. Abortion was legal. Available. His heart rate tripled.

"Kenz, please." He slipped his other hand along her face. "I'll be responsible. Whatever you need, I'll take care of it. Just, please don't..." He couldn't even form the words.

"I already tried," she whispered. "I couldn't go through with it." Her eyes slid shut, lips trembled, and then another sob bent her frame. "I don't know what to do, Jackson. I lost my job because I've been so sick. I can't make rent. My roommates are mad, and I can't tell my mother." She searched his face, pain and fear clear in her eyes. "I have nowhere else to go."

He slid a hand into her hair, an arm around her shoulders, and pulled her into his chest. His heart shattered as she sobbed against him, fists gripping his shirt as though grasping her last lifeline. Those prayers for God to move, to give him a chance at this marriage? He hadn't meant this. Never that her life would be smashed like this.

Their mistake just got bigger.

"We'll figure it out." He curled around her, cradled her close, honestly wishing, for the first time since that night in Vegas, that she'd never crossed his path. That he'd never married her.

Never ruined her life.

Chapter Eleven

(in which Jackson must figure out what comes next)

"That was Mackenzie, wasn't it?" Connor continued picking up napkins, cans, and pizza boxes.

Jackson sank onto the couch, numb and terrified all at once. Mackenzie had refused to come in. Said she wasn't up for facing people she didn't know and was going to go home to climb in bed. Letting her leave didn't feel right, but he'd had a houseful of guys.

The weight of the night pressed against him with unbearable strength, and he had no idea what to do. Staring at the blank TV screen, he saw nothing but the image of Kenzie's devastation. He leaned elbows to knees and covered his head with both hands.

"Jackson?" Sean moved from the kitchen doorway.

"Sorry," Connor mumbled, apparently only just realizing that Hank and Landon had gone, but Sean had stayed to help clean up.

"He knows." Jackson spoke into his hands, thankful that he'd already confessed his stupidity to Sean so he wouldn't have to explain the history in the middle of this storm.

"Was that Mackenzie?" Sean asked.

"Yes."

Connor set the garbage bag down and posted up on the chair near the couch. "You see her much?"

"Not since I dropped her off after Christmas."

"Did you sign the papers?" Connor said.

"Yeah."

"So...marriage annulled?"

Jackson's vision swam. "I don't know." Hadn't occurred to him to ask. Didn't really matter at the moment.

Sean also stopped picking up and sat on the coffee table. "What's going on then?"

Squeezing his eyes shut, Jackson desperately tried to erase the shattered look on Kenzie's face from his mind. Worked to replace it with the way she'd looked on the bluff in December. Peaceful. Or the way she'd looked in the backyard with his brothers surrounding her. Playful. Anything but broken, the way she'd looked tonight. Because that was his fault.

"Jackson." Connor's tone had a bite.

"I ruined her life," Jackson whispered.

"You signed the papers." Now a slice of defense—maybe suspicion—edged Connor's voice. "Did what she wanted. And you weren't the only one who got married, brother. She's responsible too. What more does she expect?"

Realizing his head was throbbing, Jackson rubbed his temples.

Sean leaned forward, gripped his shoulder. Jackson could feel the man's steady look lock on him.

"Is she pregnant?" Sean asked.

Jackson shut his eyes again. Moisture bulged in the corners by his nose. He could only nod.

Air siphoned from the room. The three men went still, and it seemed that life had come to a halt. For Jackson, for Kenz, in a very real sense, it had. This could not be rendered void. Couldn't be signed off as invalid and so easily dissolved. This was truly life altering and not something Mackenzie had ever wanted.

The fingers on his shoulder gripped harder. "God, my buddy could use some wisdom here." Sean's voice came low but sure. "Please help."

A tear slipped onto his nose, and Jackson pulled his head toward his elbows. *God, what have I done? What are You thinking? What do I do?*

As if an echo of his thoughts, Connor asked, "What will you do?"

After a long, exhausted sigh, Jackson sat back. "Be a dad? Figure out how to take care of her—of them."

"What does that mean—take care of her?"

"She's been really sick, I guess. So sick that she lost her job because she missed so many days of work. She can't make her rent."

Connor's eyebrows folded downward as he studied Jackson. "I'm not meaning to come off harsh, but, Jackson, you hardly know this girl. Is it possible she's taking advantage? Feeding you a sob story?"

"She's not Kate." Jackson turned a glare at him. "I saw the tests. All three of them. She's pregnant. And she looks pretty awful. I mean...not awful, but sick."

Connor held up his hands. "Look, I liked her fine the bit I got to know her. But the reality is, I've spent about as much time with Mackenzie as you have. I just don't want to see you get suckered."

"Again?" Jackson continued to stare him down. "Is that what you mean, Connor? You don't want to see me get suckered again?"

"No." Connor stood, frustration stamping his movement. "I'm on your side, Jackson. I'm not trying to be a jerk about this."

Jackson drew a long breath and tried to think straight.

"Maybe it's time to call it a night." Sean stood too, cautiously eyeing first Connor and then Jackson. "This is a lot to take in. Maybe sleep on it? Give yourself a chance to process and to listen for higher wisdom."

The pain in his head had become piercing. Jackson nodded, if only to have them leave so that he could shut his eyes and not have to field more questions he didn't have answers for.

"See you tomorrow, all right, buddy?" Sean leaned and smacked Jackson's shoulder.

He nodded again.

Connor paced to the kitchen and back again, fist-bumping Sean as he made his way to the door. "Right behind you," he mumbled.

Great. That meant Connor wasn't done.

Footfalls thudded on the wood floor, and then the swish and click of the front door sounded. Jackson rolled his head, looked back at his brother.

"I don't have anything else to say right now, Connor. It's a huge mess, and I haven't wrapped my head around it."

Connor pushed a hand through his military cut and nodded. "I know. I'm sorry."

Jackson turned, lay back on the couch, and closed his eyes. Waiting there in the darkness were Mackenzie's tear-streaked face and gut-deep sobs.

"I wrecked her life," Jackson mumbled again, searing guilt ripping through him.

"It'll work out."

Though he heard the cushions on the chair giving way—a sign Connor sank onto it again—Jackson didn't look.

"How do you know?"

"You're a good man, Jackson."

He snorted. "Yeah. Clearly."

"It was a mistake. You're not the first man to make that particular one."

Connor was trying, but Jackson didn't have enough in him to try too.

"You know that I have my own ghosts, so I get it. I meant what I said back home. I've got your back." Connor's strong grip squeezed Jackson's foot. "Whatever you need. Just tell me."

"Be nice to Mackenzie."

"Done." A pause passed. "I do like her. Honest I do."

Jackson was spent. Had nothing left to say. Couldn't pretend the pain in his head wasn't like a jackhammer destroying concrete.

The wood floor whispered Connor's departure. The click of the door announced that Jackson was alone.

He waited for that wisdom Sean had prayed for.

***

Are you awake?

Mackenzie looked at the words on her phone. It was early—but Jackson had told her he had a side job for the weekend, so he'd probably wanted to catch her before he went off to wire someone's house somewhere.

Yes.

How are you feeling?

Did he want the truth? She'd shown up at his front door like a half-drowned cat, sobbing a line of "I have nowhere else to go." Didn't get much more vulnerable than that. From there on out, he was getting the truth, ugly or not. Whether he wanted it or not.

Just threw up.

The three little dots at the bottom of the screen told her he was there, but an answer didn't come right away.

I'm so sorry, Kenz.

Sorry for what? Marrying her when she was too drunk to think? Getting her pregnant? All of it? Yeah. So was she. Waking up married to a stranger had been bad enough—*who freaking does that?*—but at least she could have fixed it. The lawyer had told her an annulment would be pretty cut and dried. Not a big deal.

Maybe that would have been true if she'd mailed the papers Jackson had signed. But she'd been so sick...

Now that time-sensitive window was closed. And she had much bigger problems.

A wave of nausea pinned her back to her bed. *Good grief, how long will this last?* How could she possibly carry a healthy baby if she couldn't keep anything down? She'd already been in the hospital once. A round of IV fluids—and the doctor-on-call's diagnosis, because Mackenzie had never thought to pee on a stick—and she'd been discharged with a pat on the head and a *Drink lots of fluids. It'll get better.*

She hadn't felt better, and though she'd worked in a hospital lab and knew that particular test was rarely wrong, yesterday she'd shuffled her way through a drug store and purchased a handful of her own home kits. Everyone one of them turned pink.

Denial had hit the hard face of reality, and her world had

shattered.

Kenz?

I'm here.

I have a job scheduled today, but we need to talk.

She had no idea what else could possibly be said. But yes, they needed to talk.

Okay.

Can I come over tonight? I'll bring supper. Whatever you want.

She wanted to stop puking every hour. Wanted to not feel like death would be an improvement.

She wanted to not be pregnant.

That would be okay. Nothing sounds good though. Get what you want.

Those dots scrolled again.

I'm so sorry.

Yeah, he'd already said that. Didn't change anything. She was still lying in her bed feeling awful. Still pregnant.

Something sank in her chest, and with the feeling that she didn't know how to define, the thought *You were there too. This is not all his fault* leveled off her hostile eruption.

Her phone chimed once again. *I'll call you later, okay?*

K.

Will you be home?

Don't have anywhere else to be. Bitter tears rimmed her eyes as she sent that last text. Life as she knew it, as she'd expected, had ripped out from under her. All goals, the expectations...even if they'd never really been her own. They'd defined her. Now what? She had no idea.

The morning sagged on. She heard her roommates leave for whatever they had going on. Alyssa peeked in on her to make sure she was still alive. Carmen continued to give her the sharp, icy silence of disdain. They'd given her till the end of the month to figure something out. Twelve more days to come up with the rent money she owed or find herself another living arrangement.

Which left her in a tight jam.

Mother had money. Lots to spare. And Mackenzie had a small mutual fund that Mother had created for her. But she wouldn't have independent access to that until she was twenty-five. Three years too long from that moment. But if she told Mother, maybe they could change the parameters of the fund?

That would require telling Mother. Nightmare turned terror. At this point, Mackenzie would rather spend the next few years living out of her car. That'd be interesting with a baby.

She didn't have to keep the baby. Even though she'd been unable to go through with an abortion—the choice Carmen had pushed hard for, and her failure to do it the reason Carmen now refused to talk to Mackenzie—adoption was still an option.

With that thought, Jackson's face swam through her mind. Then Helen's. And Kevin's. Something told her the Murphys would be heartbroken. All of them. Though it shouldn't matter to her—it was Mackenzie's life on the precipice of a massive crash here, not theirs—their feelings counted.

Wheel of Fortune was in the final round when her doorbell rang. Mackenzie pushed from her stomach off the couch, cold sweat making her shiver and nausea rocking her stability yet again. Shuffling to the door, she thought for a moment that whoever was on the other side might be alarmed at the sight of her, but decided caring was too much of an effort to muster. Hand on the doorframe, she fiddled with the lock and was surprised, as she had been for days now, at how much effort it took just to do little, ordinary things. Like answer the door.

"Kenz." Jackson leaned to look at her. A look of alarm washed over him, and then he pushed open the door so he could get through.

She swayed. He dropped the paper bag of whatever he'd brought in—some kind of fried food whose smell churned up the nausea in her stomach—and caught her in his arms.

It was happening again. Light dissolved into blackness, and her legs buckled. A soft groan registered in her mind—hers?—and then Jackson's panicked voice.

"Mackenzie!"

Then blissful nothing.

Chapter Twelve
(in which, Jackson proposes)

At the hospital with Kenz.

Jackson hit Send and palmed his phone. Sean would let their client know. Would explain without giving away too many personal details.

His phone buzzed back.

Praying.

He'd expected that from Sean as well. Heaven knew, he and Kenz—and the baby—needed all the prayers Sean could spare.

They'd moved her from the ER room—the large, curtain-divided space where they packed all the emergency patients until they could be sorted—to an LDR observation room. "For more privacy," the nurse had assured him, patting his arm and offering an sympathetic smile. For all she knew, he was a freaked-out husband terrified for his wife and unborn child. Which he was. Just not quite like the normal patients she certainly would have had.

An IV tube secured to Kenzie's right arm ran with cold, clear fluid. Rehydrating her. The name on her ID bracelet read Mackenzie Murphy, and he'd filled out the admitting paperwork with his information. Address. Insurance. Party responsible for payment. He had no idea how Kenz would respond to that—and wasn't sure how he'd cover the bills when his insurance rejected his claim because she wasn't listed on his account—but none of that mattered.

Kenz mattered. Lying there in a hospital bed, looking pale and exhausted, she was all that mattered in that moment.

The sound of knuckles on the wood door at his back sounded a moment before a young woman in a white lab coat and scrubs slipped into the room.

"I suspected it might be her," the woman said, her tone flat. Maybe a little harsh.

"I'm sorry?"

"Heard we had a young pregnant woman come in. Dehydrated. Checked the chart. Mackenzie's not a super common name. Couldn't remember yours."

Jackson stared at her for a moment, trying to remember the other woman who had been with Kenz in Vegas. Fairly sure this unsmiling brunette with a sharp nose and fire-filled eyes hadn't been her.

"Are you a friend of Mackenzie's?" he asked.

"Roommate."

He was actually tempted to shiver—like the exaggerated kind he'd do up on stage to make a point. Kenz lived with this? No wonder she'd shown up at his door without anywhere else to turn. Well, besides the fact that he was responsible.

"I see." He rolled his shoulders back, remembered the manners Mom had taught him, and reached forward. "Jackson Murphy."

"The dirtbag."

He drew back.

The woman perched her hands on her hips. "She tell you I've already had to take her to the hospital once?" She didn't give him a chance to answer. "You go off to God knows where to do whatever it is men like you do, and she's puking her guts out. And I'm left to deal with it."

"Carmen," Kenz whispered sharply. "He didn't know."

"Well, now he does." She glanced at the hospital bed and then drilled him with another hard look, stepping closer. "She tell you she's stiffing us on rent?"

"Carmen!"

"It's okay." Jackson brushed his fingers down Kenzie's cold arm. "How much does she owe you?"

Perfectly groomed eyebrows lifted. "You're going to take care of it?"

"Jackson." Kenzie's voice strengthened.

"How much?"

The roommate named a number that caused Jackson's heart to clench. That would more than double his monthly housing budget. Still, this winter storm named Carmen was right. He was responsible for Mackenzie's not working. Being sick. Not paying her share of the rent. He reached into his back pocket and withdrew his wallet.

"Check okay?" he asked.

"Jackson, you don't—"

He glanced down at Kenz, met her eyes. He read her misery there—and not just because she felt sick. This humiliated her.

Made two of them.

"Yeah, I do," he said.

Crispy silence crackled in the room while Jackson filled out the check and then handed it over to Carmen. The woman looked over the document like she expected to find a flaw or an *X* for his signature or something equally idiotic, and then cut a glance at Mackenzie.

"We're square. This month."

With those chilly words, she turned and left. No *Hope you feel better*. No *I'll see you at home*. Nothing but wind and bluster.

Jackson stared at the door after her. "Wow. She's pleasant."

"She's just..."

Kenz left the sentence hanging. Nothing nice to say, probably.

Still feeling the chill of the other woman, the lingering jolt of fear for Kenz and the baby, and the dizzying effect of his world having turned upside down in the last twenty-four hours, Jackson anchored a hand on his neck and shut his eyes.

Little help?

"Jackson?"

He straightened and turned to face her again.

"I'll figure out how to pay you back."

His lungs emptied, the piercing of her ache a sharp pain in his chest. "No. You won't. I don't want you to." After a quick scan of the room, he moved toward the chair near the far wall. He shimmied the seat closer to Kenzie's bed and sank onto the cushion with slow, tired muscles.

Mackenzie watched him, her face so pale and drawn that even her freckles seemed to have lost their color. Those coppery-amber eyes held on him, sheened with tears.

I broke her.

The thought was agony. He reached for the limp hand at her side, brushed her cold fingers, and then slid a gentle grip over it. "Listen, Kenz. I've been thinking about this since last night, and I know it's going to freak you out, but I can't figure another solution."

She continued to watch him, the dullness in her expression telling. It made the pain in his chest worse.

"I can't afford to cover your rent every month."

"I should get better soon." There wasn't much conviction in her voice. But she continued. "The books say after the first twelve weeks—"

"You're what, eight weeks in?"

She nodded.

"And you've already been in the hospital twice?"

A tear rolled down the side of her face.

"Kenz, this is what it is. We can't pretend that tomorrow you're going to wake up and feel normal again. And what if twelve weeks go by and you're still not good?"

Silence.

"I don't like that you're living with Ms. Hostile-Snotty-Pants." He nudged his chin at the door the other woman had just walked through. "That can't be helpful. And I can't afford to cover another month of both your rent and mine. Mostly, I don't like you being alone in this. It's my fault, my responsibility."

She sniffed. "What are you saying?"

Taking in a long draw of air, he lifted a quick prayer—or

hope—that this was the right thing to do. Not just another stupid impulse. "I have two bedrooms but no housemate. And since I've not received anything official, I'm guessing we're still married."

He paused, watched her reaction. Eyes sliding shut, leaking more tears, she nodded.

"Move in with me." Not the kind of proposal he'd ever thought he'd lay before a woman. Yet another notch of disappointing failure in his life. How his mother would cry. Still, there was something in him that lightened once the words were out. A breath of air to his suffocating lungs.

He hoped that was heaven's confirmation. This was the right thing to do.

***

Mackenzie woke up from a solid night of sleep. She'd been exhausted, even after lying in a hospital bed for five hours with an IV draining into her body. Her mind had shut down once she'd settled into bed last night. Didn't even pick at the fact that this wasn't her bed. Wasn't her townhouse.

After being discharged, Jackson had taken her home. To his place. The craziest part of that? She hadn't argued. Not even a syllable of protest.

Rolling to her side, expecting a round of nausea to hit at any moment, she rubbed at her eyes and considered the implications of Jackson's solution—and more importantly, her easy acceptance. They were still married. Now, they were having a baby. Together.

That felt bizarre. It'd been crazy enough for her to try to grasp that *she* was having a baby. But having Jackson plunge in, full force, no hesitation, hit her wonky. Not that she'd not wanted him to step up, but this was...more. And in the last few days she'd gone from fiercely independent to desperate, allowing him to take over. Make these decisions without a protest from her.

She should be alarmed. Under the exhausted gratitude she felt, she was alarmed. Being dependent on a man? Not a good way to live. Mother had warned incessantly against it.

That feeling crashed over her again. The roll of her stomach.

The icky fuzz in her head. The rush of heat. Propping up on her elbow, she hoped that she'd figure out where Jackson's bathroom was in time. Instead, she found a large plastic yogurt container on the bedside table.

Jackson whisked through the door on her third heave. He sank onto the bedside near her knees and scooped the mess of tangled waves away from her face as she lost the rest of the not-much in her stomach.

A cold sweat descended, and Mackenzie groaned. She shifted to slide her feet from the sheets, but Jackson put a hand on her legs.

"I'll empty it if you're done," he said.

"That's disgusting."

He grunted. Maybe it was a low chuckle. "I'm the middle of seven brothers. Not my first run-in with puke." His fingertips brushed over her hand as he took the yogurt container. "Tyler used to throw up every trip we made down the hill to town. Couldn't handle the blind curves. Also, remind me sometime to tell you how Matt and Lauren met."

She had no idea what that had to do with anything he'd just said. At the moment, she didn't care either. She buried the side of her head into the pillow. "Still gross."

He tucked the blankets around her shoulders and then brushed his thumb over her forehead. "I'll be back."

Footfalls whispered softly from her room and down the hall, then she heard the flush of the toilet and the sound of water running. Back at the townhouse, she'd be shivering on the tile floor in the shared bathroom, unable to make herself crawl back to her bed. Warm under the blankets, on the comfortable give of this mattress, she couldn't help but be thankful for Jackson's taking over.

Sleep cloaked her like soft velvet, and she let her worries about this deal crowd to the back of her mind. She'd get better in a few weeks, then they could discuss this arrangement again. Find something more suitable. Less...dependent. For her.

Minutes—or maybe hours?—later, Jackson's weight shifted the bed again, and she blinked into the bright light of the morning sunshine warming her room.

"Hey, sorry to wake you." He leaned to set a glass on the side table. "I just wanted to let you know I was heading out."

Her focus sharpened, and she took him in. A dark-green checked button-down was tucked into dark-wash jeans. He smelled clean—piney. An inhale of him sent her mind toward the memories she'd coddled of them playing husband and wife in the mountains.

Tucking those treasures to a safe corner of her mind, she wiggled to sit up. "You look nice."

"Thanks." One corner of his mouth tipped up, accenting that scar that managed to make him look oh-so-attractive. "I'm heading to church. Should be back by noon. I'll bring some lunch home."

"Church?" She stared at him, shocked. Shouldn't have been—the Murphys had clearly been the religious sort. But Jackson?

His shoulders rolled forward as he looked toward the floor. "Yeah. I'm one of those hypocrite messes who goes to church on Sunday." The look he peeked toward her read *ashamed*, but also, something else she couldn't define.

"Doesn't it make you feel guilty?"

"The stupid stuff I did that landed us here?" His hands folded as he leaned against his knees. "Yeah, I feel guilty. Really guilty." Again, he peeked at her. "But going to church doesn't. I mean it used to, before I got it. That it's about Jesus saving sinners, not about me pretending I'm perfect. So now? No. I don't feel guilty there. I don't go to church to celebrate my goodness. I go to worship His. Because I believe God makes messes into something beautiful in spite of ourselves."

She didn't have words. Couldn't even make clear thoughts. Jackson let the quiet rest between them. Perhaps lost in his own twisting thoughts as he gazed toward the outside world beyond the window.

What did that mean—Jesus saving sinners? Why did religious people have their own code that they thought was normal to the rest of the world?

Jackson's attention drifted back to her, and the longing in his dark eyes pulled at something deep within. It was a longing for her—but not the way she'd seen before. Not from any man—even him.

"Do you like orange juice?" he asked.

She blinked, blindsided by the abrupt change in topics. "Yes."

"I made an Orange Julius this morning." He nodded toward the bedside table. "Thought maybe you'd like some. The yogurt container is clean, in case you get sick again. And my mom makes massive batches of muffins and freezes them. Likes to send me home stocked up. So I pulled a couple out. They're on the counter, if you feel up for one."

The bed shifted again as he stood. "You'll be okay?"

"Yes."

"I have my phone. Text me if you need something. Or if there's something you feel like having for lunch."

"Okay."

He turned and strode to the door.

"Jackson."

Hand on the frame, he looked back at her. "Yeah?"

"My stuff..."

"We'll get it when you're feeling up to it. Connor can help, and if it's okay with you, my buddy, Sean. He's the guy I told you about—my running buddy. They were here on Friday night."

"So they know?"

"Yeah. They know."

A sinking feeling weighed in her chest. "All of it?"

His mouth pressed down, eyebrows pulled together, and he looked again toward the floor. "Yes."

She couldn't read his silence. But it hurt. Her gaze drifted to the window as tears burned against her eyes.

"Kenz."

She looked back to him, finding a tenderness in the look he held on her. "They won't judge you."

"What about you?" The words rushed out with more emotion

than she would have expected.

His hand anchored on his neck as he shut his eyes, inhaled, and then looked at her again. "They're messed-up men, just like me. They haven't forgotten that forgiven people forgive." His mouth lifted in a ghost of a smile. "Don't worry about me."

Mackenzie watched until he disappeared down the hall, once again wondering what those strange words meant—*sinners* and *forgiven people forgive*. Words, concepts entirely foreign to her.

How he could trust men with what he was clearly ashamed of without fearing their rejection?

Mother was right. Religious people weren't logical. But for the first time ever, Mackenzie wondered at the mystery.

Chapter Thirteen
(in which Mackenzie moves)

Kenz finally made her way to the kitchen Tuesday morning. Jackson was blending another orange smoothie when he heard her shuffling across the small space behind him. Glancing over his shoulder, he grinned.

"Morning, sleeping beauty."

She pushed a heavy mess of waves from her face. "Hi."

"Throw up already?" She'd done plenty of that in the two days she'd been in his home. The entire mystery of her appearing ghostly and landing in the hospital had vanished. Kenz couldn't keep anything in her stomach much longer than an hour.

"Yeah." Her shoulders slumped, and she leaned against the refrigerator.

He pushed the Off button on the blender and moved to stand in front of her. Lifting a hand to her shoulder, he stooped to catch her eye. "Why are you up? I can take care of—"

"You have been." She swallowed. "I mean, too much." Her gaze searched his, pleading for understanding. "I feel bad."

"Why? I told you, this is—"

"I was a premed student, Jackson. I know how procreation works." A blush colored her otherwise whitewashed face. "It's not all your fault. It wasn't fair for me to make you feel that way."

Heat touched his own cheeks. "This isn't what you wanted."

"Was it what you wanted?"

Like this? No. But someday? The right way? Yeah. He'd wanted a wife. A baby. A family of his own. She hadn't. Ever. Maybe he should tell her all that, but it didn't feel right. Felt like the fixings for a fight. Instead, he shrugged. "It's what is," he said. "And I'm willing to deal with it. To take care of you."

She blinked, and then her gaze lowered. "I know. You've said."

Her jaw shifted, and she rubbed her arm as if she were chilled. Jackson's mind was split between wanting to pull her close and wondering what she was thinking. After several long breaths, she sighed.

"I think I need to get my stuff soon. Let my roommates know that I'm leaving." She lifted her face up to his.

"Okay."

"Can you still help me with that?"

"Of course." He slid his hand from her shoulder, over her arm. "Just tell me when. And if I should have Connor and Sean there to help."

"I'll go pack today while you're at work. Then maybe tonight?"

Worry nudged in his heart. What if she passed out again? She'd be alone. Well, she'd be alone at his house for the day too, but... "Are you up for it?"

"I'll manage. Unless you have other plans for your evening."

What did she think he'd be doing on a Tuesday night while his wife was sick at home? Or sick at her place, trying to pack up her life? "No, no plans tonight. I'm usually home on weeknights—although sometimes I get a stand-up gig on Thursdays. That's rare though."

She nodded. He'd expected her to ask about weekends—to be a little curious about his other job. Or maybe share a bit about her schedule—if she had anything beyond the work she didn't have anymore.

She leaned away. "Connor and Sean would be helpful, if you're sure you're okay with it."

"I'd like you to meet Sean." He gripped her hand, not wanting her to pry more space between them. That pull tightened in his heart again, the one that longed to haul her close. Turn a little heat on whatever might still simmer between them. He wished she'd open up to him a sliver. Maybe try on the possibility of *what if.*

Her hand slipped from his, and she pushed away from the refrigerator. Gained more space. Clearly she didn't want the same thing.

Jackson stepped back, bottling a sigh.

"I made Orange Julius again." He motioned back to the blender. She'd seemed to like those. Every time he'd brought her one, she'd finished it. Couldn't say the same for much of anything else he'd tried to feed her. "Want some?"

She nodded.

"Anything else?" He poured her a glass.

"Maybe some water. I can get it though." She shuffled toward the cabinet.

"There are more muffins in the freezer," he said. "Should I get a couple out? Or, if you want, I've got a dozen eggs in the fridge. I could make some before I leave."

She shook her head. "I can make my way around if I get hungry."

"What about lunch?"

"I'll find something. Probably will be at my place by then anyway."

"You'll be okay?"

"I already told you I would be." Her voice bit a little. Mostly though, she sounded exhausted. Defeated.

Jackson watched while she turned on the tap, missing the sassy, vibrant woman he'd taken to meet his parents. The one who would have put him in his place with a whole lot of fire and snap. He missed the banter. Hopefully, that woman would resurface. Hopefully, this crushing despondency was mostly an effect of her not feeling well.

Only time would tell. But he was determined not to spend that time in apathy. A few things had settled deep and solid in his heart over the past couple of days as he'd absorbed this gigantic shift in his life. One: he and Kenz were married, and that wasn't something he was going to sign away so easily this time. And two: he was going to be a dad.

This baby didn't deserve an arctic home, even if his parents had started life together backward.

By Jackson's figures, he had about seven months to right the ship.

***

Why was he being so nice? Like, over-the-top, almost-making-her-angry nice. A slice of her wanted him to snap a little bit. So she could still be mad at him.

He felt responsible and was making good on the man he'd claimed to be. Well, he was responsible. But so was she. And the truth was, she probably wouldn't respond like he was if the tables had been turned. Especially since she had been the one to insist on an annulment, refusing any possibility that maybe they could find a way to work things out.

Mackenzie gripped the coat he'd given her while she lowered onto her bed. The room she'd spent the last two years living in was stripped. Not that she'd done a ton of decorating during her stay there—she was more of a minimalist kind of girl—but the Merit award that Mother had framed for her was off the wall and packed away. The print of the mountains that she'd purchased on a whim and hung over her bed now lay on the floor at the foot of the bed. The dresser she'd found secondhand had been cleared, and her gray-and-white bedding set that had been stripped away, washed, and now tumbled in the dryer, would be packed in a box. Likely to land in Jackson's basement. Her little life, such as it was, would fit neatly in a corner in the dark, abandoned storage. As if everything previous to Jackson had never been. Or didn't matter.

In the middle of the chaos, the mess that came from moving one's life into something unexpected and unwanted, Mackenzie sank onto the mattress and took stock. Not just of her stuff—of which there wasn't much—but of where she'd been and where she was going.

Life had been fairly easy up until last November. There was the struggle to study, yes. To be the best. But really, not a whole lot of drama. Mostly because she'd taken the path of least resistance. Mother had plans for her. Though the expectations were high—evidently unachievable—Mackenzie had worked toward them. Somehow it seemed easier than fighting. Or trying to figure out her own ideas. Her own dreams.

Did she have those?

Her eyes slid shut, and she sighed. Deep and long, her breath came and went as she brought the coat to her face. Why had she clung to this stupid coat, as if it had meaning? As if there was something there that she'd secretly wanted all along?

It was Jackson. That was why. The Jackson she'd come to know while playing his wife in the mountains. The Jackson who had awakened within her a wondering of what or who she really was.

The Jackson who married you while drunk and got you pregnant. The thought stung and seemed to have the distinct cadence of something Mother would say. The snide words also bore fruit—she set the coat aside and shored up the leaky places of her resolve.

Jackson might be the father to her unborn child, but he was never going to have her. She knew how that story ended, and she wasn't going to be that character.

Do you know how that story ends?

She knew the version Mother told. Men dominating women, robbing them of their identity, autonomy, dignity. Men refused to give what women rightfully deserved. The warning had been woven throughout Mackenzie's childhood. Emphasized during her transition to young adulthood.

Yes, she knew that fairy tales never ended in happily ever afters. Mother had given her proof. That was enough.

Mackenzie focused on the examples of women losing themselves to the dominion of men, erasing any felt goodness from Jackson. She convinced her mind and heart yet again that manipulation was at his core.

He won't have me, she whispered, glancing at the coat.

The doorbell rang, and she checked her Fitbit. A bit after six—

later than he'd said. *See, not so perfect.* But there nonetheless, and she did need his help. Drawing in a long breath, she stood, held still for a moment to let the dizziness pass, then sharpened her posture and went to the door.

Jackson waited with a to-go cup and a bag of something. A gentle smile moved his mouth. "Hey there. You're still alive."

"You texted every five minutes." She leaned on the edge of the door. "I'm not sure why you're shocked."

"That's an exaggeration." His grin bloomed full, face brightened, as if he was glad for her snark, not offended. "I was working. I set my timer for sixty minutes. Not five." He handed her the cup. "Orange smoothie."

She took the cold drink, masking her face so that appreciation wouldn't leak out. What she had for these orange drinks, she wasn't sure, but she couldn't get enough of them. And they actually stayed in her stomach, so that was a win.

Jackson rattled the paper sack. "Will you puke if we eat our burgers?" He nodded to the men coming up the sidewalk behind him.

"No promises. But go ahead."

"We could eat them out here."

"That'd be swell."

His eyebrows lifted, then he started to turn.

"That was sarcasm, Jackson. Don't eat on the front porch. You'll make my neighbors wonder what kind of person I am."

His low, rich laugh rumbled, and she tried to convince herself the sound of it didn't give her a little thrill.

"Doubt they'd wonder." He stepped through the door she held open. "They'd think it was your Frosty-the-Snow-Pants roommate and not you."

Try though she may, she couldn't bury a chuckle.

The other two men passed through the entryway and followed Jackson into the nearby living room.

Jackson's military brother paused by her side and squeezed her elbow. "It's good to see you again, Mackenzie. Sorry you're not feeling the best."

Though a blush crept toward her face, she met his eyes. What was this brother's name again? He was the one closest to Jackson. The one Jackson trusted most...

Connor.

"Thanks." She tried not to let the awkwardness come through her voice. Jackson said Connor knew the truth. How could her husband stand there, bag outstretched to his brother, acting as if this situation could somehow be normal? That it was every day a man should go move his pregnant wife from her house to his?

Jackson was not normal.

Connor reached for the burger bag Jackson extended.

"This is Sean." Jackson moved beside Mackenzie again, and the other man came toward her too. "He's my running buddy. I met him at church, and now we work the electrician-by-day gig together. Sean, this is Mackenzie."

"It's nice to meet you, Mackenzie." Sean's warm brown eyes took her in, his smile sincere. So he was playing at this move being an everyday sort of thing too.

She nodded, then tilted her head. Her view bounced from Sean to Jackson and back to Sean again. "Work and train for marathons together. You don't get tired of each other?" Mackenzie shoved the straw into her mouth, appalled that she'd be so obnoxious to a stranger.

Sean and Jackson both laughed.

"Exactly what I thought, Kenz," Connor said.

Jackson slid an arm loosely around her shoulders. "You must be feeling a little better. Got some of that spitfire back."

Honestly, he was one of a very few people who ever saw her spitfire. How he managed to draw it out of her was one mystery. The bigger one, however, was that he apparently liked it.

Instead of toying with that possibility, or acknowledging that she might like that he liked that scarcely known part of her, she held on to the fact that were Mother there, the woman would be scowling. First at Jackson. Then at her. She stiffened the posture she'd relaxed somewhere between answering the door and having three men stand in her house.

"Yes. Maybe I'm on the upswing." She left the implication of that statement linger silently, though clearly, in her glance up to Jackson.

This is temporary. I won't need you forever.

He met her look. Guessing by the shadow that passed through his eyes, he understood her perfectly. But he ignored it. Ate his burger, which did actually make her a little nauseated, and gathered the trash from the other two men.

"Point us in the right direction, Kenz." He rested both hands on her shoulders. Good gravy, he was always touching her.

She moved from his light grasp and led the way to her room.

"This it?" Connor waved a hand over her boxed belongings.

"Yes. But the bed stays. It's not mine—it's part of the rental."

"Easier still." Sean clapped his hands and rubbed them together.

"Man, this will be a walk in the park. I'd say an hour, tops." Connor smacked Jackson's shoulder. "Remember moving Kate's stuff? Ugh."

"Don't remind me. How could one woman own that many shoes?"

"Or coats?"

"Or bathroom accessories?"

"And Jacob was no help." Connor shook his head.

Jackson shuddered. "I say, if they ever move again, we contribute to a fund to hire movers."

"Ditto. They can deal with her majesty's pointing and shrieking and demanding..." Connor stopped, sealed his lips, and looked to the floor. "Sorry. I'm done now."

"Family can be interesting." Sean split the two brothers, moved into the room, and lifted a box. "Let's get to it."

Connor followed him, but Jackson turned to Mackenzie. "Any special instructions?"

"The box of books is heavy. I labeled it. Otherwise, it doesn't matter. Nothing is irreplaceable."

He nodded and held a look on her. It felt...intimate. First Sean then Connor passed them, arms loaded with boxes, and moved from the room. Jackson turned to face Mackenzie, eyes traveling over her face. His hand came up, and then he brushed the side of her cheek with the back of his fingers. "You do look a little better."

His touch rippled a wave of gooseflesh down her neck. "Oh."

"I'm glad."

"Yeah." She should stop staring at him. Stop standing there like a frozen ninny gazing into her hero's eyes.

"I'm glad you're moving to my place."

He was? *Me too.* Wait. Was she? Where was that stoic girl? The one who wasn't going to be his? She blinked, stepped away, and busied herself with the smoothie he'd brought her. Jackson closed the space her backward step had widened between them, leaned down, and brushed a kiss on her forehead.

"How about you let us get this? You can direct, okay, princess?"

Princess? That shattered her delusional step into fairy-tale-dom. She tipped her chin, looked up at him. "Don't call me princess."

Initially, his eyes widened, and he slid backward, hands raised as if surrendering. That easy, somewhat irritating grin moved his mouth. "You got it." He winked. "Yep. Definitely glad to see you've got some fire back."

He turned before she could respond, lifted a box, shot her another charming-not-charming smile, and left the room.

The effect he had on her left her wondering how much she really didn't like him calling her princess.

The answer that settled in her mind was too fast. Mother would definitely scowl.

Chapter Fourteen
(in which Mackenzie goes shopping)

She was getting a little better. Jackson reminded himself that Kenzie's color had been more often lifelike than ghostly lately, with the exception of the few times she'd thrown up. And that had lessened from the first few days.

He didn't need to hover so much.

Still, he hated leaving her alone. Had every day since the hospital visit two weeks before. The image of her passing out while answering the door, and the imaginings of what might have happened if it hadn't been him on the other side of that door, gnawed in his mind the entire time he was at work. She could have hit her head. Passed out with no one around to help her. Lost the baby. Died.

So many bad possibilities, each worse than the one before, sent an anxious throb through his veins.

But she's getting better. He focused on that rather than the disasters that hadn't happened. *She's getting better...*

Something Kenz had pointed out to him that very morning before he'd left for work. Rather sharply.

"I'm not a child you need to care for, Jackson." Irritation had sparked from her eyes as she finished her sentence by spitting his name out as if it tasted bitter on her tongue.

He'd wavered between wanting to grin—because oh, he did

like that snap in her personality, and he was ever glad to see it returning—and feeling offended. She'd rarely thanked him for his care since he'd moved her into his home. Even the minute before that little firecracker display, when he'd passed a full glass of orange smoothie to her after she'd shuffled into the kitchen, she hadn't mustered much more than a grunt.

To her defense, she had just puked. He hadn't needed to ask. After two weeks of living under the same roof, he'd seen the pattern of her sickness. She'd wake up, get a glass of water, go lay back in bed—at which point he'd begin the smoothie prep, and somewhere in the middle of his blending yogurt and orange juice, she'd vomit.

Then they'd face the awkward moment of saying good morning. Well, he felt awkward, anyway. Because he couldn't help looking at her—studying her—as he would the woman he planned to spend his life with. She *was* his wife. An attractive wife at that—even pale and face pulled into a grumpy morning scowl, her auburn hair, creamy skin smattered with freckles, and copper eyes pulled him. She was beautiful. Which provoked the longing to touch, to brush his fingertips along that smooth jawline, lose his hand within the thick waves of soft hair. Pull her into his chest, wrap her close, and whisper good morning near her ear. Maybe test those full lips from which he craved a smile...

That was how he wanted to say good morning. Mustering up a reserved grin, saying the words while making his hands and arms behave as if he were indifferent to his wife's new residency in his home, her everyday nearness, and the ever-growing attraction binding him to her, the effort of self-control made the morning awkward.

That, and not yet being able to read Kenzie's real intents. Sometimes he thought he'd feel a softness from her. Like the previous night when he'd told her that he'd had a gig come up last minute for Thursday night, but he wanted to check with her before taking it.

She'd studied him, a touch of disbelief in her look. With total sincerity in her soft voice, she asked, "Why do you think you need to check with me?"

Words that could have been glib. A means to keep him at a distance. They weren't. Tenderness had welled up in his chest, and he didn't push down the urge to touch her. He let his fingers experience the warm softness of her jawline, then neck, and the silk of her hair.

"You're my wife," he'd whispered.

At his touch, her eyes had slipped shut. The expression on her face...so tempting. But then she'd drawn a long breath, looked back at him, shifted away, and nodded. "I'll be fine Thursday night. Thanks for asking."

Door shut.

This was why he felt like a trapeze artist dangling from a still swing. Couldn't get momentum to go forward, and there wasn't a safety net on which to land.

The everyday awkwardness left him confused and annoyed, especially that morning when she'd been particularly sharp with him before he'd left for work. Beginning with that snarky response to his simple "I'll text you when I get a break." Something he'd said every workday since she'd moved in.

That morning, the one right after the night he'd nearly kissed her, she'd fired back at him. "I'm not a child...*Jackson*." He didn't think he'd deserved it, but he ducked his head like a reprimanded puppy, nodded, and finished getting ready for work.

She's getting better though. He took shelter in that thought as he forced his feet into boots. Let it calm the building irritation while he gripped his keys. Chose to be more amused with her fire than annoyed. Because it meant she was getting better.

After slipping on his jacket, he grabbed his jug of water and turned toward the door. "Let me know if you need anything."

Now cross-legged on the couch, she shut her eyes, leaned her forehead against the cool glass of half-gone smoothie, and moaned.

He decided to take that as "Okay," because after she'd already bit at him for being overbearing, he wasn't going to ask about it.

Mackenzie was a grown woman. Apparently he wasn't supposed

to worry about her, even if she was his wife. Something that would be a whole lot easier *not* to do if he could stop seeing her white faced and crumpling toward the floor. Or in a hospital bed. Or maybe it'd be easier not to feel concern if he didn't like her quite so much.

This marriage was a fragile thing. For her, he was nearly certain it was an only-on-paper thing. Wanting it to be a real, working thing and actually having that be reality were like wanting to fly and realizing you didn't have the power to do it.

Realizing you were just stuck on a trapeze bar in the middle of space with nowhere to go.

***

She'd hurt his feelings.

The door smacked shut soundly, with more force than was necessary. Jackson's footfalls clomped across his front porch, down the steps, and then muffled as he crossed the yard to reach his truck. After a moment, the vehicle door whacked shut. Again, soundly.

This time he was less amused than annoyed. Because she'd hurt his feelings.

Mackenzie brushed aside the thought, hoping the guilt of responsibility would go with it into a place of nothingness.

She didn't care. Jackson was smothering her, just like Mother had warned that a man would do. Taking her independence one piece at a time until she'd be left as a shell of who'd she been. Who she was capable of being.

Yes. That was what was driving him. His concern for her well-being and willingness to take care of her at significant cost to himself was obviously his attempt to smother her dignity and self-reliance.

Well. Maybe.

Could be the beginning. The seemingly innocuous—or even kind—start to what would become her demise as an autonomous, intelligent woman. It really could be.

Also, she shouldn't care about his feelings in any case. Any more than she should have thrilled at his gentle touch the previous evening. Or had the heart-jolt, melt-me-to-butter reaction to the words he'd whispered.

You're my wife.

Yet, even thinking them, alone and working hard to be annoyed at him, her insides did squishy things. She needed to get some serious control here.

He was making a claim on her. That wasn't a good thing.

To add bitterness to her panic, she thought about the text she'd gotten from her mother earlier that morning—the one that had crumpled her day even before she had the chance to get up and hope she wouldn't puke.

I heard from a contact at the hospital that you are no longer employed there.

Mackenzie didn't respond, which was unacceptable to Mother.

Also found out that you have not been accepted into Geffen. What is going on?

In an isolated moment of rebellious frustration, she'd texted back, *I need some time, Mother. Just let me be so I can figure some things out.*

She'd never spoken to her mother like that. Apparently Mother didn't know what to do with it, because the conversation had ended there. But as she thought back on it, more than remorse for her outburst, she felt the truth of what she'd said. She needed to figure some things out.

It was time she started reclaiming some of her independence that she rapidly—and foolishly—had allowed to slip during her sickness. She was feeling better. Some. At least able to keep down some food. Stay upright for more than twenty minutes put together. It was time she remembered this emergency landing in Jackson's home and life was not long term. Nothing more than a paper marriage she'd been forced to play out longer than she'd intended. A survival until this baby arrived.

Then...

Then?

She still didn't know. Had until the end of August to figure it out—barring any interference from Mother. Wasn't likely, Mackenzie decided. They weren't close, and Mother not checking in for months at a time wasn't unusual—a fact that was bound to be truer after that last text.

A tiny ache sprouted in her chest as her thoughts moved back to the baby. No matter how she proceeded after the birth, there was going to be disappointment for someone. Pain. Jackson. The baby. Her mother. Helen...

Ah, Helen. Jackson's kind mother had implanted herself in Mackenzie's heart and had often invaded her thoughts since she'd realized she was pregnant. Had Jackson—or Connor—told the woman she'd be a grandmother soon? Helen would be excited. Probably. Or would the timing of the pregnancy make her suspicious of her impulsive son and have her question her easy acceptance of Mackenzie?

That bothered. Way more than it should. Mackenzie liked Helen too much for her own good. And was too protective of her real-not-real husband. Yet she found herself on Jackson's couch, tablet in hand, pulling up *A Touch of Home* so she could watch more of her mother-in-law's videos. Just as she'd done every day for two weeks while Jackson was at work.

She was so pathetic.

She needed something to do.

She needed to reclaim her life.

Somehow.

That was the thing. How? She couldn't get her old job back. Still throwing up too much, and the thought of drawing other people's blood all day made her feel like the darkness of unconsciousness was closing in on her again. If she was honest, she'd say she didn't want to go back to that job even without the whole nausea-passing out problem. Hadn't ever liked it in the first place.

After watching Helen smile and talk through two tutorials, and finishing her smoothie she should have thanked Jackson for, Mackenzie closed the browser and shut the computer. It was time to get out. *Do. Something.*

Groceries.

Surely Jackson needed groceries. He ate out *a lot*. Maybe if he had some decent food stocks at home, he wouldn't. Not that she cared all that much about what he ate, but her diet seemed tied to his. Though she'd hardly complain about the smoothies. She lived on the smoothies.

Besides, she owed him some living expenses, and she had enough in the bank to help with food. Then she wouldn't feel so indebted to him. To his care.

By the time she dressed in something other than sweats and arrived at the store armed with a list she'd made, Mackenzie was ready for a nap. How long would she be so tired all the time? This pregnant gig was no joke. How did women do this?

She swept the frustration away, consulted her list, and got busy. In the middle of picking out oranges—and wow, did she really need a dozen large navel oranges?—the colorful gathering of petals in the nearby floral section grabbed her attention. She gave a second consideration to the huge bag of oranges. Her mouth watered. Yes, all twelve were definitely necessary. Those softball-sized oranges were going to be lucky to last three days through her cravings. Also, they needed more orange juice. Two quarts would be woefully insufficient. She'd get more after she visited the flowers.

By noon, Mackenzie made it back to Jackson's—back home—desperate for a glass of OJ, a slice of toast, and a nap. The last of which she'd snag quick after she unloaded the groceries and put away the three mixed bouquets. By that, she meant to arrange the stems within the unique containers she'd found at a thrift store she'd stopped at on the way home.

She had no idea what had possessed her with the flowers and supplies. Nor did she have any plan for what she'd do with the five arrangements she was already creating in her mind. Didn't matter. She soaked the floral foam while she consumed two whole oranges and a slice of buttered toast.

The afternoon slipped by. Nap forgotten.

Chapter Fifteen
(in which Mackenzie sells flowers)

Jackson slipped through his front door slightly less grumpy than he'd left that morning. Slightly, because at least at noon she'd answered his standard *How are you feeling by now?* text with a civil *Better*.

It wasn't much. But it also wasn't an *I'm not a child. Quit bothering me.* He took that as a sign—she was in a better mood.

Expecting her to be asleep, as she often was when he got home, he stopped just inside the front door, kicked his boots off and lined them up on the mud tray, hung up his coat in the closet, and stepped softly into the kitchen. First notable addition—a mound of large oranges. Holy fruit bowl, that amount would take him half a month to eat.

Not Kenz though. Apparently she *loved* oranges. Or the baby did.

Half a grin poking into his cheek, he turned to the refrigerator to find something to make for supper. 'Bout time he cooked something. This take-out business was hard on his gut and his wallet. Hadn't wanted to bother Kenz though, and given that she paled and swayed every time she smelled cooked meat, he figured the process of *cooking* the meat would be so much worse. But she'd said she was feeling better, so...

Ducking to look into the fridge, he stopped mid-bend, stared for two seconds, and then snorted. Four large containers of orange juice had taken residence on his shelves. Four. Large. Containers.

The grocery check-out person must have had a good laugh when Kenz walked away from the register. His wife wasn't showing yet—if anything she'd lost weight, which he chose not to dwell on—but given what this order must have looked like, anyone probably would have guessed she was pregnant.

He closed the fridge door and turned with a full grin, wondering what else he'd find within the hideaways in the kitchen. Surely some pickles? Several bags of chips? He moved toward the far counter to inspect the cabinets with all the eagerness of a kid at an Easter egg hunt. A flash of color caught his attention to his right, and at a glance, he stopped.

What on earth?

His eyes moved from arrangement to arrangement as he counted the flower pieces on his table. Five. Five? Who had sent Kenz five floral arrangements?

A surge of heat raged from his stomach, through his chest, over his limbs, and into his brain. Who was sending his wife flowers? What guy would send another man's pregnant wife flowers?

Easy, tiger. Get your head in the right place.

Wasn't another guy. Kenz had told him in December she hadn't dated much, and nothing serious. There wasn't anyone else. He had no reason not to believe her. So, her mom?

Yeah, that made more sense. Maybe she'd finally told her mom. Maybe her mom had reacted so much better than Kenzie had feared. Maybe all these beautiful arrangements were *I'm sorry,* and *Get better* and *Congratulations.*

Exhaling—which sounded like relief and tension all at once, even to his own ears—Jackson walked to the table to inspect the cards. Those would explain everything. Except, there were none.

A quick breath followed by a long sigh came from the couch beyond the dining room, drawing his attention from the mystery bouquets. Stretched out on his short couch, Kenzie pulled in another long breath, and then her eyelids fluttered open. She caught him staring at her, and he would have sworn her lips crept upward for a moment.

All the invitation he needed.

Five long strides took him from the table to the couch, where she wiggled to sit up. He lowered to the edge, blocking her escape, and grinned.

"Lucy, you have some 'splaining to do." He used his well-practiced Ricky voice.

Her eyebrows pulled together. "What?"

"Really? You don't know *I Love Lucy*?"

"You love who?"

"No, not *I* love Lucy." He pointed at himself. "*I Love Lucy*— the old TV show."

"Never heard of it."

"How have you lived?"

She rubbed her eyebrows and blinked. "What's *'splaining*?"

"*Ex*plaining. I'm still floundering with this revelation that you don't know this show. Are you American?"

"Do most people know it?"

"Pretty much everyone."

"Oh." She looked...befuddled? Pouty? Somewhere in between— but in the cutest way possible. Jackson chuckled.

Her scowl reemerged. "What am I explaining?"

"Let's start with the oranges. How many did you buy?"

"Only a dozen."

"How long will they last?"

"I don't know. I already ate three."

"Three?"

"Two for lunch. One for snack."

He bottled a laugh, because she scowled at him harder. "Okay. How about the small army of orange juice in the refrigerator? Will any of those survive the week?"

"Not likely."

"Have you always loved oranges this much?"

"No." She started to shake her head, then stopped. "I mean, yes. But not..."

He stretched his arms wide. "This much."

"Right."

"Okay. Last question. Who is sending you flowers?"

Her eyes widened, and she looked over his shoulder at the table.

Jackson looked from her to the flowers on the table and back again. He would have sworn that was shock in her expression. "You mean you didn't know about them?"

"Oh." She bit her lip. "No. I mean, yes, I knew. No one sent them. I…"

"You?"

"I bought… I mean I did… I mean…"

This woman was an intelligent woman. He'd seen it himself. Just, something happened right then. Baby brain? Maybe she wasn't actually awake. "You?"

"I guess sometimes I'm impulsive?" She peeked up at him.

He chuckled. "Well, that makes two of us, and explains some things." He winked and held up his left hand, on which he wore a cheap tin ring. Had since the day Kenz had shown up on his deck looking like a drowned cat.

The fact that she had yet to put her ring back on was something he'd been trying to ignore. She would. In time.

Maybe.

Kenzie's cheeks warmed to the sweetest shade of nearly red, and his fingers tingled to brush that soft skin. Instead, he looked back at the flowers. "So you're telling me you bought those?"

Looking at her hands, she nodded.

He let a playful grin slide into his cheek. "For me?"

"No."

Gripping his chest like he was in pain, he leaned back. Kenz rolled her eyes. He sat back up, and still grinning, braced a hand on the back of the couch. "For yourself, then."

"Sort of." She nudged him away, and when he moved, she swung her legs to the floor and stood. "I bought the flowers and then found those containers at a thrift store, and then I arranged them."

His mom. The pieces clattered into place. He'd left Kenz with his mom and Lauren before Christmas. Together, the three of them had done arrangements for Mom's blog. Later, Kenz had said she'd had fun. He'd taken that as a kind reassurance to his guilt because he'd left her alone with his massive family while he'd gone to town. Because she'd been a good sport about the whole married-and-meeting-his-family deal.

Apparently she'd meant she'd actually had fun.

She wandered to the table, and though he was sure she wasn't aware of it, a little smile smoothed over her expression. Jackson looked over the arrangements again, this time with a brand-new appreciation. Kenz had done a good job—and she liked what she'd produced. He was proud of her.

He reached for his phone, and after pulling it from his back pocket, he flipped the camera on and began taking pictures. One shot for each bouquet, and on the sly, a profile shot of her. Man, she was pretty, all soft and sleep disheveled and happy.

"What are you doing?" Her glance up at him was sharp.

"Huh?"

Her eyebrows raised, she nodded at the phone. "What are you doing?"

"Taking pictures."

"Why?"

"I'm sending them to Mom." He hit the Text icon and began typing.

"Stop."

"Why? She'll be impressed."

Kenz reached for his phone, managing only to snag his wrist as he shifted away from her. "Give me that," she said, a wisp of a giggle in her voice.

Oh, it was on. He lifted the phone higher and across his body, pulling her along too. "Not a chance, princess."

"I told you not to call me that." Still, laughter in her voice, and when he glanced down, a big, genuine smile on that kissable mouth.

He wrapped her with his free arm, hand spread on her hip, and pulled her to his side, pinning her there. With his other hand, he continued to text, chuckling. "I don't know why you fight what you actually like."

"How would you know what I like?" She continued to wiggle, stretching for the phone that he held away from her.

After hitting Send, he moved the phone behind his back and looked down at her. "You're smiling."

She reached around him with her other hand. "No I'm not."

"You're laughing." He shuffled his feet, making a little dance out of this entanglement as she continued to grasp for his phone, both of her arms folded around him. When he was near enough to the table, he slid the phone across the surface where she couldn't reach it and locked her in with both arms.

"Jackson Murphy!" She tried, so hard, to sound frustrated. Impossible, though, for the giggles.

"Mackenzie Murphy!" He mimicked her feigned indignant tone.

Her eyes widened, but he didn't give her a chance to argue the name. Instead, he found her waist with his fingers and let them dance over her side and belly. She squealed, throwing her head back and straining against him.

Ah. She was ticklish. How perfect.

Her laugh was like a summer river. It flowed, sometimes high, sometimes low, and he was completely washed in the delight of it. She shimmied against him, her fight against his hold only making him laugh more.

"Stop," she gasped, and he heard a pleading tone in the laughter. "I can't breathe, Jackson."

He resisted the urge to continue tickling her, not wanting her mirth to turn to frustration or anger, nor wanting her to feel truly trapped, but he kept his arms around her. She sagged against him, out of breath.

"That's not fair," she gasped.

"What's not fair?"

She looked up at him, her fists clutching his shirt, not pushing him away. "You're not supposed to know I'm ticklish."

"Why not?"

"Because you'll use it against me."

"Laughter is good."

"Torture is not."

He leaned into her a fraction. "I promise, Kenz, never to use what I know about you for torture." Dipping his head, he spoke low near her ear. "'Kay, princess?"

She tensed in his. Maybe he shouldn't push that one. But she stayed there. Didn't shove him away.

"You're stubborn," she whispered back.

"That's true. So is this woman I know. And impulsive."

"Not usually."

He chuckled. Straightened so he could see her face. Her grip loosened, but her hands stayed where they were, near his heart, and she studied him. Could she feel the rise of his pulse? See what holding her was doing to him?

"Why do you call me princess?" No trace of snark or rebuke in her voice, she asked like she really wanted an answer.

"Why do you not like it?"

"It's an insult."

"I don't mean it as an insult."

Her eyes held on him, longing and questions thick in her gaze. Jackson lowered his head, leaned into her again.

"I don't know what to think of you, Jackson Murphy." Her eyes slid closed as his forehead touched hers.

"I think you like me."

She held still.

He slid a hand up her back and then moved so that he could cup the side of her neck, his thumb grazing her jawline, fingers burying into the soft warmth of her hair. "I think you're scared that you like me."

She swallowed, and he felt the skip of her pulse against his palm.

"I think I like you too, Mackenzie Murphy." He ached to feel her lips against his. It took every reserve of self-control he had to move slow. His nose brushed hers, and her warm breath danced over his mouth.

Jennifer Rodewald

"Jackson."

He held, nearly caving to desire. "Yeah?"

Her palms flattened on his chest, and she drew a shuddered breath.

The buzz of his phone sounded from behind him. Kenz ducked her head, pulling the promise of her kiss as she shifted away.

Spell broken.

As cold disappointment washed through him, he let his hands fall. She didn't meet his gaze, looking instead at the floor.

Embarrassed? Disappointed? Confused?

He could only guess.

"Kenz?"

She stopped her slow retreat but didn't look back up at him.

"Do you really hate it when I call you princess?"

Quiet extended, and she still wouldn't meet his eyes.

"I won't anymore."

"I don't hate it," she whispered. "Not from you."

His phone buzzed again, and after a quick glance at him, she moved to grab it. He caught her arm as she went to pass him. When she stopped, he waited for her to look up again.

"I swear, Kenz. I won't hurt you. Not on purpose."

Her mouth quivered and then tipped into a ghost of a smile. "I know that, Jackson." After three more thunderous throbs of his heart, she left his side to retrieve his phone.

Making the mental shift back to texting his mom felt almost impossible when the ache for her kiss still pulsed in his veins. *Someday*, he thought, telling himself to move past it. For her. For them both—so they could have a chance at a future.

Please?

"She says they're good." A thrill painted her soft voice. Kenz stared at his phone, a smile on her face.

That was good too. If he couldn't have a kiss, a smile was much better than a scowl. He stepped beside her to read his mom's response.

Wow! I'm a good teacher. 😊 *Those are beautiful!*

The three dots at the bottom of the screen scrolled. The next moment, *Can I post them?*

"Well?" he nudged.

Kenz tapped the autofill. *Yes.*

Woo-hoo!

Then, *When will you bring that beautiful daughter-in-law of mine back so we can do some arrangements together?*

Jackson watched Kenzie's face as she read his mom's text. She stared at the screen, some kind of pain tugging her expression.

"Kenz?"

"She likes me."

"Yeah. I told you she did. Why wouldn't she?"

"It was all pretend." Slowly, she lowered the phone. "We lied to them, Jackson."

A rise of panic chased all lingering thoughts of Kenzie's lips from his mind. "No we didn't. We're married."

"But..."

"It's going to be okay." As long as Kenz didn't leave him. As long as he could figure out a way to make her want to stay.

"Does she know—"

He slipped his hand over hers and took his phone back. "Not yet."

"When will you tell them?"

A shrug was all he had. He needed to tell them. Soon.

She sidestepped from him, her fingers doodling on the table. "Are you ashamed?"

It felt like a setup. Or...just hard. Awkward. Jackson rubbed his neck, swallowed, and then squeezed himself into uncomfortable honesty.

"Of how it happened? Yes. You know I am." His jaw stiffened as he watched her blink, her chin turning away from him. Slowly, gently, he reached for her, lifted her chin. "I'm not ashamed of you though, Kenz. Not at all."

The phone vibrated against the table again. He ignored it. Kenz sniffed and reached to see the text.

Another door closed. Jackson let his hands fall to the table, tried not to let a long sigh empty from his lungs.

"She sold one."

He looked back at her, finding her staring with shock at his phone. "What?"

"If I want to sell it, that is. She said one of her followers who lives in this area wanted to know if it's for sale—and how much."

Straightening, he felt his smile return. "Well?"

She looked up at him, still in wonder.

"Do you want to sell it?"

"That'd be pretty great."

"Then tell her how much."

"I have no idea."

Jackson reclaimed his phone, typed in a quick response, and waited. Kenz continue to stare, only now at her creations. Hadn't seen that coming. His heart soared for her and with gratitude to his mom. Mom had no idea what this would mean to Kenz—that his wife could find something she liked that she could do while she still wasn't feeling all that great.

He thought of the Bob Ross paintings. Those happy little accidents.

Mom replied to his question with a figure. The arrangement being requested was in an oversized tin camp mug. He tipped the face of his phone so Kenz could see it.

She sucked in a hard breath. "Is she serious?"

"Too low?"

"No. Way more than I would have thought."

"Mom's pretty popular out there."

"But she didn't make this one."

Kenz snagged his phone again and started typing. Jackson read over her shoulder. *Hi—this is Mackenzie now, and thank you for this. But what if I did it wrong? What if the flowers wilt? Then you'll have someone complaining on your blog about your work. I would feel terrible.*

The dots scrolled again.

Did you soak the floral foam?

Yes.

Did you cut the flowers at an angle, removing all of the closed off stem at the base?

Yes.
Did you push the stem in firmly and securely?
Yes.
Then I have no problem selling this piece. And actually, I have a request for another one in your area. 🙂 *Sell?*

Jackson chuckled. How about that? "Think you'll make your money back, Kenz." He squeezed her shoulder.

By the time Jackson had made supper—a meatless pasta dish that Kenzie devoured, along with another orange and a smoothie—all but one of her arrangements had sold. Mom had taken care of the money exchange with her business, telling Kenz to set up a PayPal account the next day and she'd send the payments on.

It took them a little more than ninety minutes to deliver the arrangements. The adventure of it felt like a date, and when he offered to top it off with a stop at Chills and Thrills for a frozen custard, she didn't even hesitate.

He held her hand as they walked from the parking lot to the little diner.

Yeah. Kind of like a date.

Chapter Sixteen

(in which Jackson gets a text from his brother)

It feels like the right time.

Mackenzie let those words roll around in her mind as she waited for the vomiting to commence. Jackson had said them the night before, while they had celebrated her little stumble into floral arrangements. She'd asked him earlier if he'd told his family about the baby. While eating rich frozen custard, he'd apparently decided to circle back to that topic.

"I'll call Mom tomorrow—thank her for her help with the arrangements. And then I'll tell her." He'd waited. Watched her. "Is that okay?"

It was. Kind of. Should be more okay than it felt. He needed to tell them. But then...

What if Helen didn't like her anymore? Thought she was a tramp? Just one of those girls looking for a man to leech off?

Would Helen think such things?

Either way, did it matter? After the baby was born, everything would...

Would what? She still had no idea.

Nausea swirled full throttle, and she reached for the yogurt container that had become her best morning friend. Her stomach emptied, and the predictable cold sweat settled over her as she listened to the whirl of the blender in the kitchen.

She might could love that man for the smoothies.

Strike that. The love part.

Her world settled again, and she pushed herself upright, grabbed the puke container, and shuffled her way to the bathroom. The morning routine had become automatic. Flush the disgusting vomit, wash the container, brush her teeth, tame the rambunctious waves of her mane, and go find the smoothie Jackson spoiled her with.

By the time she made it to the kitchen, the craving for cold orange creaminess had shifted into ravenous demand. Jackson hit the Off button on the blender, shot that little grin he gave her every morning—the one she pretended didn't make her insides dance—and poured her a glass.

Thank you, Julius.

She sagged against the counter. Characteristically, Jackson chuckled. Uncharacteristically, he fingered her hair. Well, maybe not uncharacteristic. He was a touch kind of guy. But not usually so bold in the mornings, when she was scowliest.

Her mind shifted to their evening together the previous night. He'd held her hand.

She'd let him.

She'd enjoyed it.

Warmth from his body enveloped her as he leaned closer. Before she understood his intent, he pressed a kiss into her hair and mumbled, "Good morning."

What had she done? What was she doing? Even as her mind whirled, and a steady beat of panic stamped through her veins, she didn't move. Didn't say a word.

Jackson pushed from the counter, stealing the heat he'd draped over her as he stepped away, acting like nothing unusual was going on here. She held the glass to her mouth as if to drink, but didn't. She wasn't sure she could swallow.

"You're still okay with me telling my mom today?" His voice was so every day. So *Let's go for a walk. Let's grab a bite to eat. Let's hold hands like we're sweethearts.*

Let's tell my mom we're having a baby.

She nodded. Because of the couldn't-swallow thing.

He finished lacing up his boots, grabbed his coat and water jug, then pocketed his keys and phone. "Text you when I get a break."

This was the part where she should tell him to quit fussing. She was a grown woman. He'd frown, nod, and then head for the door. Everything would go back to lukewarm normal between them.

Except she'd apparently decided to skip that part of the morning routine.

The warmth of him fell over her again, and he'd brought along that piney scent that she'd so enjoyed while wearing his sweatshirt, or when she'd curled up next to him in that horrible pull-out bed. Her eyes slid shut before she understood how that might be perceived by her husband, standing just right there. His large, rough palm cupped her face, fingers slightly bent as they found their way into her hair again. Her breath snagged, and she forced her eyes up to him.

He had waited for her, watched her with a silent request.

What if...

What if she gave in to this attraction?

Curiosity—and maybe a strong dose of yearning—nearly had her tipping her mouth to his. Because what if the farfetched possibility of *them* could really happen? What if he was always like this—so tender yet funny? Stubborn but gentle? What if his taking care of her never felt like him running over her?

What if she actually liked having him call her princess? Like she was *his* princess?

Mother would be appalled. Full-blown, screeching-lecture mode. Staging a dangerous-behavior-breaking intervention. This was not who she'd raised Mackenzie to be. Not how she'd taught her daughter to think.

The pause extended, and Jackson accepted her silent refusal. Instead of bending to catch her mouth, he pressed another kiss to her head—this time her temple.

"Think you'll create some more beauties?" He stepped back, but his hand stayed lost in her hair. The depth of whatever he felt lingered in his eyes.

"Maybe."

He smiled. Looked like pride. Made her feel...special.

"Send me pictures. I'll send them on to mom. Or—" His head tipped to the side, and then he reached for his back pocket. "Better yet. Send them to her yourself." He texted something and then pocketed his phone again.

She missed his touch. And also, he wanted her to text his mom? "You're telling her today?"

"That's what we talked about."

"Then maybe she won't—"

"Kenz."

She looked at his chest. Then to the floor.

"She'll be happy."

Then why was he afraid to tell her?

Because this compatible ease wasn't going to last forever. They didn't have a real relationship built on anything other than a crisis born of mutual stupidity. No one could build a life on that. Especially when she hadn't wanted it in the first place. Sooner or later they'd both have to face reality. In that moment, she realized, perhaps for the first time, how much the end was going to hurt.

Perhaps his mind skipped to the final, painful chapter too. He turned away without another touch or another softly spoken word and left.

***

Jackson stared at his phone.

It was time. Although, he'd have to admit he was a bit of a liar. It didn't feel like it was time—even though that was exactly what he'd told Kenzie last night. Sitting there working out how to tell his mom that Kenz was pregnant felt like something he wasn't up for.

Sitting on the back of his vehicle, backed into a parking lot near the deserted walking trail, he scanned the late-winter scene. At home, there was probably snow. The higher elevation and more northern location allowed for the white stuff. Here, the landscape rested in a drearier greenish-brown. Spring was nearby though, and with it would come a rush of colorful change.

Change was definitely coming.

Jackson rubbed the back of his neck, feeling the cold weight of his phone against his palm.

Just make the call.

Mom would be happy. He knew she would. So this hesitation was all him—because he knew the truth. The marriage, the baby...products of bad decision-making, enhanced with way too much alcohol consumption and inflamed by a ridiculous amount of self-pity. He would always know that reality, and it would always needle him.

Which meant the relationship he would have with his mom from here on out would be stained with the fact that he was now both a failure and a liar. And he had thought taking her pity about Kate had been bad enough.

If he came clean with her—and with Dad—would his relationship with them change? Because this constant need to cover, to pretend, had already grown tiresome, and he was only three months into a long haul of handling the consequence of one stupid night. Telling the whole truth was tempting. But also terrifying.

How could I have done something so dumb?

Also, there was Kenz. He liked her. So much. And the baby... He wasn't exactly sure how he felt about that—other than responsible. But he was relieved to know he'd actually get to hold his child. Thinking about the alternatives that Kenz could have chosen knifed deep in his heart, and he was thankful she'd chosen this road, even if it was awkward.

She'd made a hard choice. Did the hard thing. Time he man up and do the same.

He'd tell Mom. All of it. And pray Mom would still accept Kenzie as she had done before, because there was a clear connection his wife had made with his mom, and he was certain Kenz needed it. Especially with the obvious strain she had with her own mother—a woman Kenz rarely spoke of, and when she did, it wasn't with great attachment. In fact, she hadn't told her own mother about the baby, and he doubted she'd told her about him either.

Ugh. Maybe he wouldn't tell Mom all of it. Risking Kenzie's dignity that way wasn't worth it.

Jackson lifted the palm in which he'd held his phone during his mental debate. It was just a simple phone call. Just...

Do it.

He tapped her contact info and made the call.

"Jackson, how are you?" Mom always answered like she'd been hoping he'd call. She did with everyone. One of her charms.

"I'm all right, Mom, thanks." Did he go with small talk first? He had thought this through. Had a speech planned out. One he couldn't remember. "How are you?"

"Well, I'm thrilled to see your Kenzie liking floral arrangements. She really did well with those creations last night. Has she been practicing?"

"Not that I know of. I came home from work last night, and there they were on the table." This was good. A natural ramp to what he wanted to say.

"Really? She just decided to make some all the sudden?"

"Yeah, well, she's had some extra time on her hands and felt well enough to do something with it yesterday."

"Well enough?"

"Um, yeah. Kenz has been pretty sick lately." Perfect. Go from there. Except, his mouth dried up, and his pulse raced, and the right words got lost somewhere between his brain and his mouth.

"Sick? Oh no. Is she okay?"

"Getting better."

"Is it serious?"

Life changing. But that wasn't what Mom meant. *Just out with it.* "Kenz is pregnant, Mom."

Dead. Silence.

"Mom?"

"Wow, son. I'm...shocked."

She sounded shocked. But not in a bad way. Still, he felt his heart sag.

"Yeah, we were too." He tried to keep the defeat out of his voice.

"Oh, Jackson. It'll work out. You'll see. Even if it's not how you planned, one look at that little one, and you won't be able to imagine anything better. I promise."

If she only knew. He could tell her. Should.

"She's been pretty sick, huh?" His moment of opportunity slipped by as Mom carried the conversation forward.

"Very sick. Been in the hospital twice because of dehydration, and she lost her job because she couldn't go in."

"Can they fire a woman for being pregnant?"

"Probably not, but she didn't realize that's why she was so sick until after the job was gone."

Mom held quiet for a moment. "Still, seems like it shouldn't have happened..."

"I know." He watched while a pair of geese landed in the creek beyond the walking path. Wondered how long the gander and goose had been together and if they had a nest they were preparing nearby. "But it did, and I'm not sure she really loved her job anyway. In any case, she's just starting to function again. So your selling those arrangements last night was kind of huge. She was so happy. Thank you for doing that."

"Ah." Her smile gleamed in her voice. "I'm glad to know that. You tell her if she wants to keep creating, I'll keep posting her work. Would that help you two?"

He had yet to see a bill from the hospital, but without a doubt knew it'd be in the thousands of dollars. Money he wasn't sure he could scrape together. But they were talking about Kenzie's work. Kenzie's money. Not his.

He envied the calm simplicity of those geese across the way.

"That'd be great, Mom. I gave her your number, so you might hear from her."

"How about you send me her number, and I'll call her myself?"

Kenzie would like that, wouldn't she? Knowing his mom, she'd say something about the baby. Maybe Kenz wouldn't like that. He couldn't know for sure. Didn't know his wife that well.

There was something so very wrong with that.

"Jackson?"

"Sure. I'll send you her number."

"Should I not mention the baby?"

"No, it's fine. I told her I was going to tell you today, so she knows." Hopefully, it was fine.

The pair of geese floated on the water, ducking under to snag a snack and staying close to one another. What would that be like? Just to be together naturally?

It'd be like the few hours he and Kenz had last night. *See, not impossible. Not farfetched.*

"Jackson, are you okay?"

"I am." He rolled a grip on the end of the tailgate, considering this second opportunity to be straight with his mother.

"It's a lot of change at once, isn't it?"

"You could definitely say that."

"We'll be praying for you and Kenz, then."

"Thanks." They needed it. So much more than Mom knew.

The phone call ended, and he breathed a small amount of relief. At least the awkward part was over. Unless, of course, he decided to be honest.

Maybe sharing all the details wasn't necessary. Maybe keeping them just between Kenz and himself—well, and Connor and Sean—was fine. Right, even.

So maybe the worst was really over. He could look forward instead of back, work on what he felt was conceivable between him and Kenz. In the end, it was possible that no one else ever needed to know why they'd married in the first place.

He went back to the old house he and Sean were rewiring with less of a cloud shadowing his day. Last night had been a good night for Kenz and him. That morning had been pleasant. Her response to his text at lunch had been *I'm going shopping again. Flowers.* Which was so much more than *I'm fine* or *Better.*

Things were looking up. By the time he fist-bumped Sean at the end of the day and walked away with a "See you bright and early for a long run," he was actually whistling some tune he'd heard somewhere.

His phone buzzed as he loaded his tools in the truck, and he checked it before he hopped into the cab, expecting it to be Kenzie.

It was Jacob.

A baby? In a hurry to prove something?

The tune died on his lips. Hadn't thought Mom would tell *everyone* just yet. He swallowed the ball of heat in his throat and texted back.

Most brothers would go with something like "congratulations, bro."

Sure. Congrats.

Then, *Guess we know why you eloped.*

Jackson felt like something exploded in his head. *What?*

There are ways to prevent that. Or did you miss that day in health class? Classic Jacob. Thought he was funny, when really he was just a jerk.

Must have. Want to explain it to me?

Too late now. Kate's gonna die.

Why would Kate care? *Sounds like your problem. Not mine.*

You think? Kind of think you did this on purpose. Just to shove it in my face.

What on earth? *Shove what in your face?*

Anger and confusion whirled through his mind. What was Jacob's deal?

No answer.

Forget it. Like it mattered anyway. Jacob always did whatever he wanted—it never mattered to him who he ran over to make his end game. Whatever was going on between him and Kate was probably something they both deserved. Jackson wasn't involved.

He tossed his phone onto the seat across the cab, hopped in, and started the truck. When the phone vibrated again, he ignored it. Didn't need to know.

That resolve kept until he walked into a silent home and found a note on the counter. *Delivering some flowers.* 🙂

He sighed, happy for his wife and thankful to his mom, even though he was also annoyed that Mom somehow thought that telling Jacob about the baby was a good idea.

Wished Kenz had waited for him to go with her.

The phone buzzed again. Maybe it was her.

Hope your shotgun marriage lasts.

His hand shook as heat raced through his limbs. The urge to throw the phone against the kitchen cabinets nearly won over.

Run. He needed a run. A hard, body-crushing, mind-numbing run.

Chapter Seventeen

(in which Mackenzie doesn't know what she wants)

Helen had sold three for her this time, and Mackenzie walked back into the house with enough money to cover next week's groceries. A giddiness bubbled within her, making her unable to stop smiling even if she'd wanted to.

Also, Jackson's mom had been just as he'd promised. Over-the-moon excited about the baby. That had mattered so much more than Mackenzie had realized. Not only for her but for Jackson.

Having spotted his truck in the driveway, she entered the house expecting to find him in the kitchen. Instead, a high-pitched whirl drifted from the basement. The treadmill. He didn't usually run on the treadmill. Especially when it was nice out. Had told her it was a little hard on his knees, and the calibration of pace and distance were off, so he only used it to train during bad weather. Also, he ran in the mornings, often with Sean.

Curious, and a little selfishly bummed that he hadn't had a smoothie ready and waiting for her with an eager "How was your day?" greeting, she opened the doorway to the stairs and began the descent. How very quaint would that scene have been? And ridiculous. What was she thinking?

The screech of the belt pitched higher. Faster. How hard was he going? It sounded...

She peeked around the corner of the stairwell to see him near the opposite wall. The basement was pretty much empty, except the pile of her boxes in one corner, his desk, and the treadmill near the opposite exposed brick wall, along with a few free weights and a gray yoga pad. Jackson ran. Like a man on fire.

"Hey." She raised her voice to a near yell, hoping she wouldn't startle him and cause a wreck.

He kept going. Sweat ran down his face, soaked his shirt front and back, and glistened on his legs. The contortion of his expression was more than focus. It looked like pain. And yet he pushed harder. Bumped up the speed on the flat-screen control and moved faster.

Something told her this wasn't just a run. Perhaps it was the tension in his jaw. Or the scowl she'd only seen on her husband's face a handful of times—every one of those times he'd been unhappy. Very unhappy.

"Jackson." This time she did shout.

He glanced over. A flicker of surprise passed through his eyes, but that was it. No smile. The amount of disappointment she found in the lack of his grin took her off guard.

She'd wanted his smile. Wanted his banter. Maybe a little of the whatever it was that he'd left her with that morning.

What she got was a frown, then he jerked the stop cord, and the machine slowed. His chest heaved as he panted, his legs slowing with the pace of the belt, and when he stopped, he stepped off and gave her his back, turning to grab his water jug from the ledge of the foundation wall.

"Going pretty fast there."

His shoulders heaved with his body's demand for more air, and he glanced back at her. That was it.

"Didn't you run this morning?"

Grabbing the towel that was waiting on the yoga mat, he shrugged. She stepped toward him, unsure if she was getting upset with him for being so jagged or if she was worried.

"What's going on?"

With both hands, he wiped his face with the towel, then swiped his neck and hair. He didn't meet her eyes.

Both. She was both irritated and concerned. "You're not one for the silent treatment."

"You know that for a fact?"

She sucked in a breath as her heart rate kicked up. His banter didn't often have the flavor of snark. Not anymore. What was this all about?

Tempted to snap back, she kept her words even instead. "What did I do?"

He scowled. Then looked toward his shoes, jammed a hand through his hair, and shook his head. "Nothing." His eyes found her again. "I'm sorry. You didn't do anything."

Dropping the towel, he moved toward the stairs, but before he passed her, she gripped his drenched arm. Still breathless, he stopped, and the look he narrowed on her was a fierce storm.

An ache bloomed near her heart. For him, for whatever had plunged him into this turmoil. She lifted her hand from his arm and feathered her fingers over the stubbled shadow along his cheek, then with the pad of her thumb, she traced the scar on his top lip. His breath released into her palm, warm and moist, and his gaze intensified.

He moved, stepped into her, one hand sliding over her neck, the other at her back. When his mouth lowered to hers, it wasn't with timidity. He kissed her with hunger, pulling her into him as if she was the antidote to whatever plagued him and he was desperate for her.

She held stiff in surprise for only a moment before she melted into him. His heart pounded hard into her palms, and hers sped up to match the pace as he walked her backward until she met the wall, his kisses giving and taking equally with hers. Her hands slid over the dampness of his shirt, explored the sweat-soaked hair above his neck, and roamed the arms that held her.

He pulled away as suddenly as he'd begun, his breath once again ragged. Now hers was too. One hand slipped away from her as he straightened and leaned his arm to the brick wall, head to his elbow. She felt him tremble against her and looked to find his eyes shut, brow furrowed.

"Jackson?" Her voice caught on his name. Part longing. Part confusion. The hand that still held her waist moved, and then he caressed the side of her head, fingers burrowing into her hair as he seemed to like to do. After a long, controlled exhale, he opened his eyes.

"I'm sorry," he whispered, breath still labored.

For...that kiss? For being grumpy two minutes ago?

She fingered the scar above his lip once again, and once again his eyes slid shut.

"What happened?" Before. And now. Why was he upset? Why'd he stop kissing her?

"I need a shower. And a clear head." He pushed away from the wall, from her, his thumb running the outline of her cheekbone before his hand fell away. "We can talk after?"

Tempted to grip that nasty, sweaty T-shirt and tug him back into an instant replay, she rolled her fingers into her palms and nodded. "Should I make something for supper?"

He shook his head and stepped away. "We'll go out."

And then he disappeared up the stairs.

***

Jackson let the hot water pelt his shoulders until it turned cold. This pattern he had somehow established—being upset and letting it build in his head until he acted out with impulse—he needed to get a grip on it. Hadn't he already made a big enough mess with that kind of handling?

Man, that kiss though. Kenz had gone with him into the passion, and it had been so tempting to take all that she'd be willing to give. She was his wife, after all.

But they needed to get some things solid between them. Soon. This whole dangling-on-an-emotional-trapeze thing wasn't working for him, and maybe if he didn't feel like he was forever on the brink of failure when it came to this delicate marriage, his brother's text wouldn't have dug into him so deep.

After shutting off the water, drying, and tossing on a clean set of clothes, he sank onto the edge of his bed and leaned his head into one hand.

Was this even possible? Wanting something real between him and Kenz felt both hopeless and desperate.

He was trying to do the right thing by her, by their baby. That should count for something, shouldn't it? But he was also trying to smother the reality of what he'd done, hoping nobody else would ever find out what had happened in Vegas, how stupid and reckless and impulsive he'd really been. That wasn't exactly noble. More like cowardly.

I get it, God. And I'm sorry. Truly, I'm sorry.

Why didn't he feel forgiven?

There would always be someone like Jacob. Someone who would rub his face in it. Who would take his deepest shame and hold it fresh under his nose. Worse, someone who wouldn't even flinch at tossing blades toward Mackenzie as well. Taking Jacob's crap was one thing—and clearly he didn't handle that super well. Having it fall on Kenz? Intolerable. Jackson would lose it.

A knock clunked hollow on his bedroom door.

"Jackson?"

"I'm about ready."

Kenz waited for a breath. "You dressed?"

He stood. "Yeah."

The door slipped open, and she peeked around the edge. "Are you..." She bit her bottom lip, hand still on the knob. "I was just worried..."

He closed the space between them, pushed a smile onto his mouth, and bent to kiss her temple. "Sorry. About all of it. I was upset, and I shouldn't have—" He sighed. "I hope I didn't scare you."

She hadn't seemed scared by his sudden, passionate outburst. Then again, he'd been pretty much all in his own head, drowning in emotions he'd let rage beyond control.

"You didn't." She sounded small, and her gaze drifted to the space between their feet.

"Kenz?"

She inhaled and then looked up at him like she had to force

herself to do it.

He swallowed, a fresh swell of shame rolling through him. What if she'd thought... "I'd never—"

"I know." Her hand covered his bicep, small, soft, and warm.

He wished he could read her. Understand what was making her shy from him again. Why she was acting like something between them had gone wrong.

"I trust you, Jackson." She brought her eyes back up to meet his. "You're a good man."

Her words, so delicately spoken he wasn't sure he'd heard correctly, were such a massive contradiction to what he felt that he barely kept the crash of brokenness within himself. Afraid to speak, because if he did, he might crumble, he stared at her, waiting for her to retreat.

And she did. Her hand slipped away, and she stepped backward into the hallway before turning toward the front room.

Jackson inhaled, blinked, and rolled a fist. She had no idea what she'd just done—how much deeper she'd pushed the desperate longing for her into his heart.

Please help.

After two more controlled breaths, he followed her to the front door, and the chilly air outside aided his focus.

In the truck, he asked where they should go. Pasta. She thought she could handle pasta. He found a little off-the-beaten path Italian restaurant, and they kept the conversation light through the meal. Feeling more like himself and less like he was about to drop into an abyss, he thought that maybe he'd just let the whole thing go. Maybe they didn't need to have a serious talk after all.

Kenz wiped her mouth with a napkin, her gaze falling to the table before she spoke. "What happened earlier?"

Guess she thought they needed a real conversation. Jackson slumped back onto the booth, debating what and how much to tell her. His silence lasted too long.

"Was your mom upset?" she said.

"Not at all."

"I didn't think so. She called me—was happy."

Should have guessed Mom would call Kenz. "She must have posted more of your work too."

"She did. Three sold. I was delivering them when you got home."

He nodded. "I saw the note."

"Were you mad that I wasn't home?"

"What? No." He looked at her, knowing that he scowled. "Is that what you think of me? That I'm a control freak?"

Her expression remained steady. "No. I mean, I hope not."

"I wasn't mad about that, and you're not my prisoner. I'm glad you're feeling up to doing more now." He sat up, rubbed his neck, and then dared a touch of his fingers on her hand resting across the table. Her hand stayed still, neither grasping his nor withdrawing. Searching for what he really wanted to say, all he could come up with was a simple attempt at the truth. "I want this to work, Kenz."

It took a breath for her to make eye contact, and when she did, she looked scared. But it was out there, so he might as well go all in. "This marriage—I want us to work. Not just until the baby comes, but—"

She looked down, eyebrows tugged inward. Same move he'd seen when he'd tried this *what if* quest with her right after Christmas. The pinch in his chest cinched harder with each breath. Her silence spelled out her answer loud and clear. Again. He slid his hand from hers, retreating into himself. Unsure what to do, he folded his fingers together and searched for something else to say. Anything. Because five to six more months of this dead-ringing silence would kill him, and she looked just as miserable.

"I was thinking." He tried for a lighter tone. "After I talked with Mom today, that you haven't been to a doctor yet. Have you?"

"Just the hospital." Her voice sounded painfully strained.

"We need to get you in somewhere. Have any ideas?"

She shook her head.

"I could ask Sean to ask his wife, if that's okay?"

Face fixed toward the table, she didn't answer.

"Or maybe you want to check around yourself?"

Her shoulders moved as she drew a long breath. "Jackson, I'm not sure I can afford—I mean, I have insurance, but I'm only twenty-two, and I was a student so it's my Mom's policy, and..."

"I already told you I'd take care of this." He still wasn't sure how. Had been waiting for a steep hospital bill, certain his insurance wouldn't cover anything for her. Full prenatal care? He had no idea what that would cost but was certain it would be expensive.

"I'm not on your policy," she said.

"I know. I'll make some phone calls."

"No one will cover maternity when I'm already pregnant."

"Maybe. Maybe not. If I can prove we've been married since November, maybe someone will be sympathetic. Besides, I think there're some new laws regarding prenatal care..."

"I don't want to go on Medicaid."

"I'm not suggesting that, but if it means you get good care, and that's what needs to—"

"No. I'll go back to work. Find another job."

"You're just starting to get better. And anyway, I just told you, I'll take care of the bills. This is my fault, so—"

She met his eyes, sparks in her gaze. "Stop doing that."

"What?"

"Acting like I can't make decisions. Like I'm not a grown woman who can handle things for herself."

He stared at her, feeling like she'd slapped him. "What do you want from me, Kenz?"

Her bottom lip trembled, but she continued to glare.

"I don't know what to do here, so you're going to have to help me." He leaned forward, whispering, though his voice felt harsh. "We're married. This baby is mine. You lost your job because of this. Aren't trying to get into medical school anymore. I feel like I've wrecked your life. But when I try to help, to take responsibility, you get mad. So I'm just..." He ran a hand over his neck, let his gaze flicker to his hands before he forced himself to look at her again. "I'm stuck, Kenz. What am I supposed to do?"

A sheen glazed those copper eyes, and again she fixed her attention to the table. When she sniffed, his shoulders folded inward. Defeated. They both felt it.

Though he was unsure he'd be welcomed at her side, he slipped from his bench over to hers, and when he wrapped his arms around her, he was a little shocked to have her huddle into him.

Nothing about this dinner had cleared up anything between them, other than to highlight that it was complicated. Everything about their marriage was complicated. *She* was complicated, and he was nearly certain that unless she let him in, he'd never understand why. Sometimes he doubted she understood herself. But he held her, pushing down his own confusion and frustration. He curved a palm over her head and leaned to whisper near her ear.

"It'll be okay."

In truth, he had no idea how any of it would be okay.

Chapter Eighteen

(in which Mackenzie goes to a doctor)

There weren't a whole lot of other options. Jackson's offer was the best one, and she hated that she needed to depend on him so much. She'd owe him. Already did, and had no idea how she'd make it square.

But he was right. She was having this baby, and she needed medical attention. It was the responsible thing to do. After arguing with herself about it for two more days, she made her first appointment. Later, she told Jackson over sandwiches. A week later, to be exact. A week of trying not to remember how his passionate kisses had stirred longing in her belly. A week of denying that she wanted to feel it a hundred times all over again. And a week of battling the press of guilt because she knew he felt every bit of distance she fought to replace between them since that night.

Hormones. Likely. Just hormones on overdrive, messing with her thoughts and emotions.

Jackson had controlled his reaction to her announcement about the appointment. Stopped chewing, watched her with a maintained neutral expression, and then nodded. Did she want him to go with her? he'd asked. She'd given her name as Mackenzie Murphy on the new-patient registration questionnaire. Needed his insurance information, though she was certain that would be useless. Was also certain Jackson, too, thought his insurance would deny them a prenatal claim, but he wasn't saying that.

No, she didn't want him at the appointment. That would not help keep the distance she'd fought to maintain.

Again, he nodded. This time no eye contact.

She felt selfish.

"You'll tell me what the doctor says though. Right?" The look he lifted to her was pleading. It hooked into her heart in a way that was both painful and endearing. He worried about her. Had even before the baby. She had the coat and boots to prove it.

She'd never considered how safe it would feel to have a man be concerned for her well-being. Safe. Not...condescending. Not insulting. But safe. Why would that be?

Still, she fought the gap closing between them.

"Kenz?"

"Yes, I'll tell you."

"Everything? Promise me, Kenz." Still a pleading tone. Not demanding.

"I'll tell you."

He nodded. They finished their Saturday lunch. Went on to do their separate things—she spent the afternoon looking up new trends for floral arrangements and texted his mom to ask about her thoughts on a few things she'd found. Like succulents in wooden boxes. What kind of soil was best for that? How would Helen protect the container for the most longevity? She made a list of what would be needed. Threw up somewhere around four, which was becoming less common as the days moved forward. Then researched costs for succulent arrangements. After, took a nap.

Jackson spent his afternoon in the basement at a desk he'd moved from what had become her room. Working on new material, he'd said. Needed two or three new sets to polish off a fresh performance.

He was booked for that night. Showing at eight. He'd leave around six. This was normal for their Saturday nights. Mackenzie had initially liked that he was gone. She hadn't gone along. Hadn't ever seen his act. Though curious, she doubted she ever would.

The empty house gave her space.

Lately, though, the space had begun to feel like too much. She'd hardly own that out loud, however. Jackson had a TV, and she watched movies while he was gone. The time he was away in those evenings was her only chance to watch, really. He didn't turn on the TV much, except for a basketball game here or there. Otherwise, the screen remained blank. He was a reader.

That had surprised her. Evenings together were quiet. Him with a book or a magazine. She would find one too. Over the weeks, she had moved from the confinements of her room to the shared space out front. He read on one end of the couch. One day a few weeks back, she'd landed herself on the other.

That had felt like the right amount of space. At least, before the kiss. Since, when he was gone in the evening for a show, she missed his quiet presence on the other end of the couch. Missed hearing his deep, quiet chuckle every now and then. Missed having the opportunity to glance at his profile and admire this man who was now in her life.

The appointment happened. All was well, and though sorry for the sickness that Mackenzie had endured, her doctor said she felt confident the worst was behind them. She used the Doppler to find a heartbeat, and the moment Mackenzie heard the rapid swish-swish-swish, something in her chest squeezed. That was a life. A tiny, new life growing in her belly.

That thing in her chest was amazement—and that surprised her. She'd studied biology. Knew the facts. But this...

This was immediate. Personal. Her life. And a new life.

And Jackson's.

He should have been there. She could imagine his reaction and hated that she'd missed seeing the wonder play out on his face. Hated that he'd missed the marvel of hearing their baby's heartbeat for the first time.

This was not normal for her. But she couldn't overcome the

bond she felt for the man she had entangled her life with. He was kind to her. Gentle and not overbearing. Not like anything Mother had warned her about.

As much as she'd tried to ignore it, deny it, sever it, this twining of her life with Jackson's was real. And though terrifying, she found herself not only reconciling to that truth but tempted to embrace it.

Where would that lead?

The following evening, Jackson asked about the appointment.

"Everything is good." Mackenzie forked spinach, a strawberry, and a clump of feta cheese into her mouth.

"You're sure? The doctor said you're okay?"

She didn't miss that he asked if *she* was okay. "The baby is good. I heard the heartbeat."

His eyebrows jumped, excitement dancing in his eyes. "Yeah?"

A chuckle lifted from her lips. "Yes."

"What was that like?"

Oh, he should have been there. "Kind of amazing, actually." Could he hear the wonder that filled her?

He grinned, a thrill bright in his eyes. His hand slid across the counter where they sat and covered hers. "And you're both okay?"

Caught in the warmth of his gaze and the moment of shared amazement, she turned her palm to meet his, and he wove his long fingers with hers. "We're both okay," she said, unable to fight the draw between them. "She said the worst is behind us."

His shoulders relaxed, but the grip on her hand tightened. He lifted it and brushed her knuckles with his lips. As tingles spread across the skin of her hand, she shut her eyes and let herself imagine, just for a moment, what this moment would be like if they were a real couple. The way he wanted.

The idea felt less terrifying every day. Which was, paradoxically, alarming. Sometimes. Other times, like in that moment, it was peaceful. Like coming home to a place she'd never imagined, and finding out it was exactly where she belonged.

"The next appointment will be the ultrasound." She found his gaze already soft on her and squeezed the fingers that still held her hand. "You should come."

"Yeah?"

"If you want to."

"You know I do."

"Yes. I know you do."

"Do you want me to?"

Her hand untangled from his, and she lifted her palm to his face. Cupped his jaw, let her thumb trace that scar she'd come to like so much. "I want you to be there."

When he leaned, nothing in her panicked. He kissed her forehead. Paused. Her nose. Paused. She tipped her mouth, and he found her lips with a gentleness that unfurled warmth over her face, then flushed through her body.

"I wouldn't miss it," he whispered.

They finished the meal. Books in hands, they landed on the couch. Him on his side. Her, next to him, head tucked on his shoulder.

Just the right amount of space.

***

What happened to my socks?

Jackson chuckled as he read Kenzie's text. Leaning against his vehicle while his heart rate settled into something closer to normal after his run, he replied with his thumb on the screen and a grin on his face.

I have no idea. Tell me.

Jackson Murphy! Every pair I own are sewn together!

He laughed again, imagining her adorably exasperated face. Man, he wished he were home right then. *Wow. That's crazy. Wonder how that happened.*

A Bitmoji of her head exploding lit his screen next, followed by *I NEED a pair of socks!*

Go look in my room.

You're suggesting I dig through your underwear drawer?

Nah. Should be some at the end of my bed. What he'd give to see her face in the next minute.

What's this? Her text came with a picture.

Yep, just as he'd left that morning, his bed neatly made, and fourteen new pairs of socks lined out on the edge.

Happy sock day, he typed.

She didn't answer for quite a while. Honestly, that didn't surprise him. He was learning that when Kenzie didn't know what to do, she often went with silence. That was okay. But then...

A text came through. She sent him an emoji. A heart.

Jackson felt like he'd won the Boston.

***

Could it be happening?

He watched the creek across the walking trail. The pair of geese swam over the glassy water. Together.

He'd looked it up. Geese mated for life.

As always, no matter where he was or what he was doing, his thoughts found Kenzie within near reach. Her belly was beginning to swell. Showing the baby growing within. Theirs.

His. And hers.

The pull in his heart every time those thoughts turned in his mind was strong. An ache, and yet an amazement. He kept praying, asking for the miracle of a mess turned beautiful. A mistake brushed perfectly into part of a bigger, extraordinary picture. For God to Bob Ross this marriage.

And maybe it was happening.

The weeks between that outburst of angry passion and this quiet, soft kind of existence with Kenzie had expanded. Next week, she'd be five months along. They'd go to the clinic, and together they'd glimpse for the first time the secret life growing within. Just the other night, as she'd leaned against him while they read, she'd sucked in a breath. Alarmed, he'd let the book in hand fall, sat up, his arm around her, and searched for pain on her face.

"I felt it," she'd breathed.

Her hand splayed over the lower part of her stomach, still mostly flat. The swelling he could spy was only visible when she wore her tank top and boxer shorts. Only when he glimpsed her beautiful morning profile.

"Really?" The urge surged to cover her hand, to search with his own palm for the stirring she'd felt. He gripped her shoulder instead.

Wonder had caught her eyes, making the copper shine like a new penny. She smiled, soft and warm.

"What's it like?" he asked.

She bit her bottom lip. "Like something rolling. Or brushing inside."

"Does it hurt?"

"No. Not at all."

"Tickle?"

"Maybe a little. It feels..." With the back of two knuckles, she feathered a touch against his abs.

He sucked in a breath, and his stomach muscles clenched. Did she know she was killing him with this?

Her touch fell, a shyness dimming the marvel in her expression before she looked away. "It feels like nothing I've ever felt."

She knew what her touch did to him. Felt bad for it, because she didn't mean to stir the things she stirred in him. Did she?

He had settled onto the couch, pretended to be unaffected. Sitting back too, though not leaning against him as she had been, Kenz also returned to her book. He'd expected the next night that she would have sat on the other end of the couch. Reopened the space between them she continued to maintain.

She hadn't.

A spring breeze stirred the trees over the creek, drawing his attention back to the present.

The geese continued to swim and bob. Bob and swim. Sometimes distance would splay between them, the gentle ripples lapping in the open water that spread from gander to goose. Slowly, almost imperceptibly, the pair would drift back together. Each did their own thing. Bobbing for food. Paddling against the lazy current. But they were together as well.

Maybe it was happening with his marriage. Slowly. Quietly. Almost imperceptibly.

Leaning against the sidewall of the bed of his truck, one booted foot propped up on the tailgate, Jackson let hope drift in his heart. And he prayed, as ever, one more time.

**

Kenzie's doctor was nice. Young. Enthusiastic. And ignorant about the kind of marriage that existed between him and his wife.

Thank heaven.

Dr. Knapp shook Jackson's hand, called him *Dad*, and congratulated him. Standard bedside manner, Jackson supposed. Still, it was a bit of a thrill.

Jackson slid onto the chair beside Kenzie, emotions all bundled up and acting crazy inside.

"Are we ready for our first peek?" the doctor asked. The mobile ultrasound had been wheeled into their room, complete with a monitor and a bottle of gel the doctor had lifted from the cart and was now shaking.

Jackson's heart pulsed with an oozing throb, like he was about to bungee jump off the Golden Gate Bridge. Not that he'd ever done that—didn't even know if one could. Maybe it was more like the way his body buzzed before a race or a show. All nerves and adrenaline and excitement.

Kenzie looked over at him, lifted a shy smile, and then nodded to the doctor.

Dr. Knapp smiled. Squirted bluish gel on his wife's exposed belly.

"It's warm," Kenz said.

"Yes." The doctor chuckled. "I'm not into shocking my patients." She winked and then turned a smile to Jackson. "You missed the Doppler last time. Want to hear the heart?"

"Yes."

She flipped a switch, applied the funny-shaped thingy to Kenzie's gelled stomach, and then...

Swish-swish-swish...

Jackson smiled, his hand finding Kenzie's as he trained his gaze on the monitor. Kenz squeezed his fingers, then hers were laced with his and together they watched the screen.

There it was. Their son or daughter. A little head, with alienish eyes. A nose. A chin. Two hands, complete with fingers, one at its little mouth, sucking its thumb. Tiny legs were bent and crossed.

Jackson leaned forward. "Hi there, little one."

And then the little lima bean stretched.

"Ah." Dr. Knapp's tone smiled. "Your baby knows your voice, Dad."

He had no words. None. Just this feeling of total awe. And overwhelming love.

The showing was not long enough, though the doctor toured them through all the vital parts of that little miracle growing in Kenzie's womb. Everything measured well, looked good. She congratulated them both, told them what to expect the coming month, gave instructions for the next appointment, and then left them alone in the room.

Jackson found Kenzie's eyes. He could hardly breathe as, with one palm, he covered the bare place on her belly where their baby hid. Kenz watched him, and when he stood, then leaned, she kept the intense connection between them. He hovered over her.

"That was amazing," he said.

A tear slipped from the corner of her eye. "It was."

He lowered his head. Brushed his nose against hers and then found her lips with his. She responded with a feather light kiss of her own.

It felt real. Everything between them, in that moment, felt real.

Chapter Nineteen

(in which Jackson has a bad night at the club)

It was hard to keep reality straight. Especially when she felt with him what she felt.

Mackenzie lay in her bed, hand splayed over the place where her baby grew. The exact place Jackson's large hand had touched in the doctor's office last week.

She could not pry that moment from her memory or erase the way his intimate look had plunged into her heart, making warmth race into the very depths of everything she was. If she dared a word for that expression, it would start with *L* and be four letters long. She didn't dare. Love was dependency. It was a liability. She'd been raised not to fall into the trap. Not to need it, not to want it.

Independence was the god of her upbringing. Men were idols against it. *Gratify your physical thirsts if you must, Mackenzie. That's what the pill is for. But keep yourself out of it, here.* Mother had tapped her heart. Then her head. *Mind over emotions. You'll thank me, I swear.*

Rebellion seemed to be in Mackenzie's heart, because though she didn't dare name it, she knew what longing was and what that longing was after. Mother would give her a grave look. *The trap is set,* she would say. *Are you so simple that you will fall into it?*

Mackenzie sighed. Mother. She was a brittle, crispy woman.

Not entirely unfeeling, but purposely detached. Often Mackenzie wondered why Mother had ever had her at all. She was not unloved by Mother—never would she go that far—but the emotion part of love had been...tamed. Carefully trained not to rule. To behave in a mild, orderly fashion. Mother had expectations for her daughter, plans that would make Mackenzie successful, prominent. Comfortable.

Happy?

As the spring morning sun grew stronger, the songs of early birds drifted through the window. Mackenzie shut her eyes and peered into the future her mother had laid out for her. Medical school. Residency. Fellowship. Finally, full career. Department head somewhere...

The view drained the life from her. She hadn't wanted any of it.

She'd enjoyed books—not the medical journal sort. Long walks through the park. Quiet places where she could settle her thoughts and not be required to answer questions and strive to be the smartest in the room. Studying had always been a heavy burden, the hardness of it never balanced by any kind of enjoyment in the task.

She liked the flowers and plants Helen had introduced into her life.

She liked the quiet, unassuming life she'd stumbled into.

And Jackson. She wiggled her toes, encased in the new pair of socks he'd cleverly given her, and sighed.

Her husband was possibly the kindest person she'd ever met, even when she was frosty to him. Trouble, yes—in such an endearingly innocent way. And he could banter with the best of them. But always, under the volley of words, was a kind spirit. A gentle heart—one who seemed to offer himself to her.

The temptation of it grew daily. For a moment, while lying there in the stream of yellow sunlight that poured across her bed, she let the unfamiliar imaginings of that life take off. Pictures of couples she'd seen from a distance floated through her mind— hands linked, faces soft with smiles. A small child running to and from them. An idyllic view that Mother had proclaimed to be a farce.

The couple became Jackson and her, the youngster theirs. They looked happy.

Do not imagine those moments exist behind closed doors. The memory played of a sharp response given to her twelve-year-old self the one time she dared to question Mother's view on those *couples.* Her face had been so hard, eyes so angry, Mackenzie hadn't pushed on the subject. Never asked again.

Grandmother had once said Mother's heart had been damaged and would never again know softness. Mackenzie never asked for details. Only accepted that Mother must know of what she spoke.

But Mackenzie and Jackson lived behind closed doors. He smiled at her behind closed doors. Was kind and gentle behind closed doors.

The contradiction made her dizzy. She'd been dizzy far too much the past five months—she didn't need to let her imagination add to it. Propping up on her elbow, then rolling to her side, she paused, wondering if she'd vomit before she began her day.

Her stomach behaved.

A whirl from the kitchen beckoned her to come forth among the living. She wasn't nearly as sick as she had been, but Jackson continued to make her smoothies, and she continued to crave them. Fingering her hair into a pile on her head as she left the room, she wandered down the hall, skipped the bathroom, and entered the kitchen, where he was doing exactly what he'd done for months.

He smiled at her, and when she came nearer, stopping to lean a hip against the lip of the counter, he shut off the blender.

"Good morning, beautiful." He'd done that lately—called her beautiful. Since the ultrasound.

She couldn't scowl at him for it. She liked the sound too much.

With one small step, he closed the gap between them and pressed a kiss near her hairline. He'd been doing that too, in the mornings. Sometimes at night before bed.

She inhaled, long and slow, to savor the piney scent that drifted from his freshly showered body. This had also become common, everyday for them.

"How was your run?" she asked.

He moved to fill a glass for her, then passed it from his hand to hers. "Good. It's beautiful out today. The sunrise was stunning."

The sunrise was a favorite event for him. He mentioned it often.

She lifted the glass. "Thanks."

"You're welcome." His hand lowered, paused midair, and then he covered the small swell of her womb. "How are you this morning?"

That was new. He hadn't really touched her, aside from the kisses to her forehead, since the doctor's visit. There was a fluttering within, and she couldn't tell for sure if it was her or the baby's response.

"I think we're good," she whispered.

"Didn't hear you throw up."

"No. Not yet."

"Two mornings in a row?"

She smiled. The fluttering happened again, directly below the warmth of his hand. "I think the little one hears you."

"Yeah?"

"Feels like it's doing flips."

Oh, that smile. She could puddle onto the floor.

His hand left her belly, drifted toward her face. With a tender softness, he touched her cheek and then stepped away.

If they were one of those couples she'd imagined that morning, she'd follow him, close this ever-present space she fought to keep between them, and test the refuge of his arms. Perhaps check the softness of his mouth.

"I was thinking." Jackson cut off her musings, and good thing for that. "It's so nice out. We could have lunch at the park together. Unless you don't have time? Or maybe you don't want to."

"At the park?"

"Yeah." He smiled, teasing. "You're allowed to eat outdoors, right?"

She squinted. "What?"

"Such a city girl." He laughed. "We call it a picnic. Don't worry—the wild animals will not get you."

"You're such a pill. I've eaten outdoors before."

"You have?"

She rolled her eyes. "I just meant what park. I haven't seen a park nearby."

His chuckle tempted a smile on her lips. She did enjoy that deep, quiet laugh of his.

"I'll pick you up." He gathered his water jug, cell phone, and keys and paused to drop a quick kiss on her head. "Bye, beautiful." Then brushed her abdomen with his fingers. "Bye, little one."

And then out the door.

Reality was really hard to keep straight.

***

What a stupid night.

It had happened before. There were people wandering this planet that Jackson couldn't make sense of. The woman at the club hadn't been his first encounter.

Still.

He pushed open the front door, hoping Kenzie would still be awake. If she wasn't, he'd probably run, and hope the belt of the treadmill didn't wake her up. But he'd rather see her. It would ground him. He was coming to terms with that—the fact that he'd fallen for the woman who was his wife, and simply being with her made his life better.

Love. That was what was happening. He loved her—and though he'd been praying for their marriage to work, the truth of love sort of shocked him. Perhaps because he'd never felt something so strong, so deep.

The sound of a movie met him as he stepped into the house. A good sign. He slipped his shoes off, lined them up on the mud tray, hung his jacket, walked to the kitchen, and deposited his keys.

He found her curled up on the couch, wrapped in a soft

blanket, watching a movie he vaguely recalled from the previous decade. Something his mom had watched, probably because it looked like a chick flick. A little surprising. Kenz didn't watch those, that he'd seen.

"Hey."

She sat up, smiled. "Hi. How was your gig?"

"Pssh." He dropped onto the couch, shoulders heavy.

She wiggled to sit up. "What happened? New material not go over?"

"No, it went over fine. Thanks for letting me use us, by the way." He'd asked her permission while they'd picnicked at the park the week before. It was golden material, really. How many couples actually got married in Vegas the way they had? Too good not to use, but he absolutely wouldn't have if she didn't want him to.

That day, under the sunlight filtering through the dancing leaves in the park, she'd examined him after he'd asked her. As her gaze searched, the connection between them grew ever more tender. "Are you sure?" she'd asked. "I won't be there, so it doesn't really affect me. But you? You'll be completely exposed."

"Not completely. I won't tell *everything*." How could he? Hadn't even had the guts to tell his parents. Besides, most stand-ups were given to exaggeration, and everyone knew it. Even if he did tell an audience that he'd married a woman he'd never met while on a weekend trip in Vegas, they likely wouldn't take him seriously.

The double edge of being a stand-up. People didn't take you seriously whether you wanted them to or not.

On the couch, Kenz shifted closer, and one small hand warmed his shoulder, bringing him back to the present. "Tell me about it."

"Brian—my manager—loved it. Said we need to record the new material before spring is over." He glanced down at her, relaxing a bit under her attention. How good did it feel to have someone—her—want to hear about him? Sit there and listen like she thought what he had to say was important? "I did a set about finding out you were pregnant—playing the honeymoon-baby angle. How it took so long to realize you were pregnant because *What? We just got married!* The multiple pregnancy tests, and how you'd bundled them up in a sandwich baggie to show me. But then I was like, welp, some of us just *jump into it.*" Their glances met, her eyebrows raised. "Yeah, I took a few liberties on that story. Anyway, rolled with it so it was funny. The audience loved it."

"So it went well?"

"Right. I mean, the audience laughed. But then, after the show, I was hanging around, meeting people. Brian says it's part of the job, so I do it. We had some of last year's CDs, and I was at a table signing them. This woman steps up from the line, and I'm like, hi, person I don't know...blah, blah, blah, making small talk, and all the sudden she goes, 'I want your autograph.' I shrug. 'Sure.' She turns, hikes half her tiny skirt up over her bare hip, and points to her white half-moon." He shivered. Covered his eyes. "I was like 'Lady! Did you miss the last like thirty minutes of me talking about my *wife?*'"

Silence. For like forever, Kenz just sat there in silence. Then she snorted. The most unrefined and unexpected snort-laugh he'd heard.

"Are you serious?" she said.

"Think I'd make that up?"

"I don't know. You're a good storyteller."

He pinned her with a glare. "I would *not* make something like that up, Kenz."

She kept laughing. "Does this happen to you often?"

He shrugged. "I mean, sometimes. But I was just talking about my pregnant wife!" He pounded the last sentence out, careful to emphasize each word like it was its own point.

Kenz chuckled on. He dropped his head into his hand, his fingers forked into his hair. At least she wasn't mad. This was not what he'd expected from her—but way better than her being mad.

She nudged his shoulder. "Come on. You were flattered."

He turned, looking past his shoulder to peer down at her. "I was horrified. I stood up, hands in the air like there was a gun aimed my way, pointed to my ring, and then walked."

While laughter still danced in her eyes, she poked out a pouty lip. "It must be hard for you to be so sexy."

Oh. So not letting that one slide. He leaned into her. "You think I'm sexy?"

A blush filtered over her face, the amusement slowly changing into something so much more serious. And tempting. The distance between his nose and hers closed.

"Tell me what you think, Kenz."

Her hand cupped his face, fingertips grazed his jawline, thumb feathered his top lip. The playful mood between them shifted.

"Mackenzie?"

She pushed into him, her mouth meeting his.

Her kisses were sparks and flames, igniting a blaze that had been coal smoldering between them. He surrendered to the heat, everything else forgotten. Then she was in his arms, and he was moving them from the couch.

He wanted his wife. And she wanted him.

***

She studied his profile while he slept. *Her husband.*

They'd been here once before—though she couldn't remember all of it. This was how she'd ended up pregnant in the first place.

A shiver rippled over her shoulder. She brushed her palm over her bare arm, as if to chase the chill away. Jackson rolled toward her, eyes still closed, and gathered her against him. His warm breath fanned over her forehead, and then he pressed a kiss near her hair.

"I love you, Kenz."

She squeezed her eyes shut.

What had she done?

Chapter Twenty
(in which Mackenzie rebuilds distance)

By the time he'd come home from his run, gotten out of a shower, and dressed, Kenz had vanished. Not just from his room. From the house.

Not a word. Not a note.

A pain moved in his chest—something like a warning and a disappointment at once. He pushed it away. Reading too much into the silence. Assuming things that were likely not true. Yet he'd exposed himself, was now completely vulnerable. The trapeze pulled higher, his grip on it strained.

By lunch, he began to worry. She'd answered his text with *Running some errands.* That was all. No ETA. No response to his reminder that he was booked for another gig that night.

She's running.

The two words slithered in his mind, sank cold and heavy in his heart.

Why?

Why would she run? He'd laid out everything. Wanted desperately for her to know his heart, his hopes, his intentions. Him. And to be blunt, she'd initiated the intimacy. He'd been careful to be sure of her willingness.

Confused and heartsick, he breathed in relief when she came home twenty minutes before he needed to leave for the booking.

"Hi." He stood from the couch and met her near the kitchen,

taking a bag from her arms.

"Hi." Her eyes flitted to him and then away.

He waited. Nothing.

"Did you get everything you needed?"

"Yes."

Pressing his lips together, he watched her. Waited. She busied herself, unloading the supplies she'd gathered, and a bag of oranges, a jug of juice, and two large containers of yogurt.

The silence pressed too hard. "Did you eat at all today?" he asked.

"I got a sandwich at the deli." She glanced at him from her place at the fridge. "You didn't wait for me, did you?"

"For a while." Man! Her retreat hurt. Maybe she was still unsure of him, thought that his desire was only physical. He moved closer, slid a hand to her back.

She stopped moving. Her shoulders sagged as she exhaled.

"You okay?"

Her stare pinned on a spot somewhere between the floor and the refrigerator door.

"Kenz...." With two fingers, he lifted her jaw, forced her to look at him. "Last night—"

"I'm okay." Her mouth lifted in a way that seemed forced, and she laid a palm against his chest. "We're good."

What did that mean?

"You have a gig tonight, right?"

He nodded, his mind in tangles, heart lost.

Leaning into him, she lifted to kiss his cheek. "You'd better go, then." And she moved away.

What was happening? He stared at the spot where she'd just been. Picked through the expressions he'd watched play over her face. None of them what he'd hoped for.

All of them distant.

Maybe he was reading too much into it. Expecting a shift in things between them when he shouldn't have. He could take her at her word. She was good. They were good. At the moment, he didn't have a better choice, because he had to go, and sifting through the pieces of the day—all of which felt jagged and sharp—would drive him nuts.

"I'll be back before midnight." He turned, swiping his keys from the counter as he moved to face her again.

She nodded.

"You'll be okay by yourself?"

"I'm always okay by myself." There was a bit of bite in that.

He ignored it. Closed the gap between him and her, leaned over her shoulder and kissed a freckle near her eye. *Love you.*

He kept that bottled within and left with a much safer "Good night."

***

She was hurting him.

It had never occurred to her that men could be hurt, which seemed like a bizarre revelation. Men? They did the taking, the trampling, the hurting. Wasn't that the warning? The trap her mother had preached against?

But the look on his face. She literally felt his pain.

He'd get past it though. Wouldn't he? If she showed him that she just wanted things to step back to the way they were two days before, he'd be okay with that.

He had to be okay with that. She couldn't give him more.

***

The gig had been uneventful. Exhausting, but uneventful.

Brian had asked if he was feeling okay. "Just don't seem as animated tonight," he'd added.

"I'm good," Jackson lied. He then buried the sting of Kenzie's apathy toward him. Good thing he'd had practice. Middle kids were notorious for being overlooked. Never had it been intentional, but he'd gotten lost in the crowd of his siblings more than once. Had learned to suck it in and swallow it deep.

He swallowed hard. Many times over during the evening.

The house was dark and silent when he got home. On autopilot, he slipped his shoes off, lined them up where they belonged. Hung his coat. Deposited his keys. Glanced at the couch where Kenz had been the previous night.

Empty.

Wandered to his room, stared at the bed they'd shared.

Empty.

A breath left his lungs. Defeated. Angry. Hurt. Kenz had lied—they were not good. Searching his mind over, trying to understand her reaction, he found only the silent sting of her rejection. Alone, he stripped down to the sleeping essentials and slipped between the sheets, feeling the hope that had surfaced over the past few weeks sink.

Though he loved her, she didn't want him. Not for real. Not forever.

This marriage painting looked like a cold, lonely, disaster. Apparently it was going to stay that way.

Chapter Twenty-One
(in which Jackson meets Mackenzie's mother)

"Talk to me, buddy." Sean lifted his water bottle, squirted a stream into his mouth, and then tossed it into the bed of the truck. "You've been running mad, working silent, and brooding for a week. What's going on?"

They'd run a brisk twelve miles. Jackson's recovery time wasn't as quick as Sean's. Never had been. He gulped in a few more long breaths, trying to calm the charge of his heart rate. "Just tired."

Sean held a look on him. The knowing kind. Then pressed two palms against the side of the truck and leaned down into a deep hammy stretch. Jackson followed, letting the quiet between them flow. Water rippled behind him, and he glanced at the creek.

There they were. The inseparable pair, starting their day together as the sun began to warm the wooded area around them. Watching the geese, the hurt within Jackson billowed. Burst.

"We made love." Quite an opening. Everything in him felt raw and exposed and wrecked.

Sean glanced at him, one eyebrow lifted.

"Last week." Jackson stood, jammed a hand into his hair. "I swear, it was mutual."

Standing, Sean just listened.

"Since, she's given me her back. I mean, she pretends everything is fine. Everything is like it was before—which was not bad at all. But—"

A pause extended.

"But?"

"It's not fine." Gripping the lip of the truck bed, Jackson leaned back, looking up to the wakening sky. "God, I can't do this." He shut his eyes, let the cry he'd just ground out shoot toward heaven. Strength suddenly gone, he bent his knees, lowering into a squat on the blacktop of the parking lot.

Sean stepped closer, and one hand squeezed Jackson's shoulder.

Hands buried into his hair, Jackson fought for a steady breath. "I told her I love her. Gave her all of me. She...ignored it."

The morning chatter of birds joined with the soft ripple of water and a gentle breeze. They filled the painful silence.

"Maybe she's not rejecting you." Sean squatted beside him.

"I don't know what else it is she's doing."

"She's still with you."

"Because she has nowhere else to go."

"I doubt that. She's smart, ambitious. Educated. Likeable. She could find something else if she wanted to."

"Then what? Why, when I tell her I love her, do everything I know to show her, would she intentionally put distance between us?"

"I don't know." The loose gravel scuffled against the blacktop as Sean moved to sit. "But I've seen you two together. When you bring her to church. The few times we've gone out. Never once did I get the impression that she didn't want you. Instead, Misty and I both thought she very much did want you, but she seems afraid."

"I've made it very clear that she's safe with me."

"What if her fear isn't about you at all?"

Jackson tested that thought. Honestly, everything in him hurt too much to let logic or reason really take root. But he'd tuck it away to consider later, in the lonely hours at night when his thoughts would shout into the silence.

He dropped to his backside, let his feet slide forward, and wrapped his arms around his bended knees. "I'm in over my head.

Sean, I really don't think I can take this."

"Would you rather she left?"

Man. Sometimes, in his angriest moments, he thought if he could forget her—forget the hope of *what if*—his life would be easier. But then an emptiness would drop in his chest. So deep and lonely and silent, it actually made him a little afraid.

"No." He'd rather the pain than the emptiness.

"She needs you, Jackson. I doubt she knows what love is. She wants to, but she just doesn't know."

Maybe.

He wasn't sure he was the one to show her. Like he'd just shouted to heaven, he really didn't feel like he could do this. Didn't even know how.

"What if it doesn't work out?" Jackson glanced at Sean.

Sean nodded. "It might not."

Silence.

The minutes ticked on, and a rumble in his stomach reminded him that he needed to get going for the day. Home. Shower. Smoothies for two. Work. The rhythm of his life—a beat that he hadn't minded two weeks before. That night had changed everything, and not how he'd wanted.

He stood up, and Sean followed. Another clap on his shoulder stalled him from leaving.

"I'd wager, Jackson, that even if this ended exactly how you're afraid it will, you'd regret not putting your heart out there. You'd always wonder what would have happened if you chose to love her no matter how she responded."

Jackson winced. "Think I'm brave enough to do that?"

"Yeah." Sean met his look. "Yeah, with some God-filled courage, I think you are."

***

The dreams were bizarre, yet she couldn't remember them. All she could really pinpoint was that she woke up lonely—not just alone, as she had most of her life—but lonely. It was a new level of loneliness, like she'd known something other, something beautiful and safe, but she'd fallen away from it, and the isolation consumed her.

It made her confused and grumpy. And sad.

Surely this was all just pregnancy madness. Hormones gone haywire. Emotions on a bungie cord.

Jackson moved in the kitchen. She heard the familiar beat of his morning routine, and the craving for an orange smoothie made her mouth water. In spite of the distance she'd re-established, he continued to act in kindness. Though she could read the questions, feel the pain he wrestled with in the glances he'd cast on her, he didn't lash out.

It was like she was testing him. And he was solid against the blows.

She couldn't be testing him. She wasn't that...shallow?

But if she was testing him, he was surprising her.

The whirl of the blender stopped. She could stay in her room, avoid him for the morning. For most of the day. Wouldn't be the first time.

Lonesomeness pressed harder. And also, the craving.

She caved to both. There he was, dressed in jeans and a T-shirt, ready for work and pouring her a glass. Her heart pricked when he glanced over his shoulder.

"Good morning," he mumbled.

"Hi."

"Sleep well?"

"Sort of."

His brows pinched. "No?"

"Weird dreams."

The gap between them closed. His move? She couldn't say for sure.

"Bad?"

"No. Just weird. I actually don't remember them."

The gaze he settled on her was like an offering for her escape. All she had to do was move into his arms. He'd take her. Hold her.

Love her.

Why was that so terrifying?

She lifted the glass he'd slid in front of her. "Thanks for this."

"You're welcome."

They paused. Stuck in awkwardness again. Like being trapped in sinking sand, slowly going down, unable to escape the pull.

He'd love you if you'd let him.

Her heart moved in response to that quiet whisper. The shift felt both painful and dangerous. Her mother's voice stamped over the words she'd just thought. *He'll take you. All of you.* The way Mother said it was bad. Always.

For a moment, she imagined Jackson taking her. All of her.

It didn't feel bad. Not in her imagination.

"You okay?" Jackson tipped his head, studied her face.

"Yes." She pushed away the webs spinning through her mind. "Like I said, just tired."

"Okay." With two steps he was at the sink, rinsing his glass. Then he gathered his water jug, his keys, slipped on his boots, and moved for the door.

He stopped, hand on the knob. The pause felt weighted, and the gaze he turned to her beckoned. She met his eyes. Maybe she shouldn't have. Too much emotion there.

"Bye, beautiful."

Her heart split as he walked out the door.

***

The battle raged inside him.

It'd be easier to avoid her. They could live as passive near strangers. Cohabitate like indifferent neighbors under the same roof. It would work. It'd be safer. Easier.

But Sean was right. Jackson would always wonder what might have happened if he'd been bold enough to push through the pain.

Still, he'd taken the Thursday night gig, claiming that they could use the money. It wasn't a lie. The bill from the hospital visit in January had arrived, the damage summitting in the thousands of dollars. Thus far, insurance wasn't playing nice. Every extra gig was a godsend.

There was a corner in him, though, that understood what was what and wouldn't lie about it. Taking the extra work was him avoiding home. Avoiding her. Because that meant she'd be safely asleep when he got in. Out of sight...

Never out of mind. No matter what he did.

He crept through the dark house. As he reached the threshold to his room, a sound, barely discernible, but loud enough he couldn't pretend to ignore it, drifted from her room.

Just the whisper of sheets as she shifted probably. *Or she's crying.*

Not likely. He summoned ice and iron to his heart. Either way, wasn't his problem.

Suffocating the whisper of conscience, ignoring the God-given urge to care and protect, he entered his room and readied for bed. As the cool of the sheets settled around his waist, he shut his eyes and willed himself to be temporarily deaf.

The sound came again.

He rolled to his back and sighed. *No.*

Heaven spoke. Not with words, but he understood plainly. *No.*

His ears rang. Heart hammered. Mind tore.

Another sniff.

God, what are You doing to me?

With a flick of one hand, the covers flung to one side. He planted his feet on the cool floor and moved forward.

She didn't answer his tap on the door. He knocked again and then slowly pushed the door open. The smell of *her* assailed him. Warm orange blossom and clean mint. His head suddenly felt light, while his mood felt heavier.

"Kenz?" he whispered.

"I'm fine." Her voice faltered.

He moved forward, then crouched beside her bed. His fingers found the mess of her thick hair, and he traced the locks until he could feel the outline of her jaw, then her nose, her cheek.

"You're crying."

"Just a dream."

"Again?"

No answer.

"What was it?"

"I don't know."

Was that true? Was it worth pushing? A fresh tear slid from her eye onto his thumb, and he submitted to the demanding sense that she needed him, even if she didn't want him. He stood, rounded the bed, and slipped in between the sheets.

"What are you doing?" As she rolled to face him, she sounded breathless but not alarmed.

In the darkness, he searched for the silk of her hair and then drew her head into his chest. "Holding my wife." His voice strained, the words painful as he pushed them past his lips.

She lay stiff against him. "Why?"

He couldn't say why. Not because he didn't know, but because it would hurt too much to speak. He said nothing.

Slowly she softened against him. The silence in the darkness broken only by her soft sniffles. When he felt a warm dampness soak into his T-shirt, and the curl of her fingers gripping the fabric near his sides, a single tear leaked from his own eye.

Why was this so hard?

***

Mackenzie woke up missing him.

He'd held her through the night but woke early to go for his run.

It was dangerous, this missing him. This reliance on him. Her upbringing rose up against it. And yet.

Lying on her back, she sighed. She'd lied to him last night, about the dream. This time she remembered.

She'd left him and the baby. Walked out the front door after saying she was done, and he'd let her go. The burn in her chest was like the furnace they used to melt glass, and her heart had reshaped into something hollow. In the dream, she'd looked back at him.

Devastated. His look. Her heart.

Dependent relationships were the antithesis of the extreme independence she'd been taught to grip. Why would she be devastated to walk away from one? Yet though it was just a dream, she could hardly stop weeping.

What was Jackson doing to her?

She rolled to her side, propped herself up, and mindlessly laid a palm over her undeniably pregnant belly. Seven months. Two more to go. Still, no answers beyond.

This had to stop. She had to find a way to end this madness before she was snared and only regret would span before her.

Mother would be the antidote. Jackson wouldn't stand a chance, and even if he endured a meeting, he'd not sign on for a future knowing that would forever be a part of his life. Perhaps it was time to meet and let the collision of ideals make their mark.

Feet solid on the floor, Mackenzie fought for the resolve to do it. Until then she'd avoid him.

***

He'd been shocked more than once in the last twenty-four hours. First, to have Mackenzie not only tell him that she wanted to tell her mother everything but also that she'd like him to meet the woman.

But now...

Wow.

Colleen Thornton was her own little hurricane. All wind and piercing rain. Damaging and reckless. Their lunch meeting had lasted all of twenty-minutes.

He would never forget it.

"You had plenty of other options, Mackenzie. And yet you've waited until now to come to me. And how dare you bring him along?"

He'd seen Mackenzie's pulse leap, the pounding of it fierce on her neck. His fists curled inward as he tucked them in his lap and leaned into the table. "She wanted you to know. Wanted you to meet me. There's no need for this anger, Mrs. Thornton."

"Ms." Sharp green eyes stabbed against him. "Ms. Thornton. And this conversation doesn't require your input."

"Kenz is my wife. I won't stay silent while you rail at her like that."

"Mackenzie is my daughter, and you are out of your place."

He reached under the table for her hand. It trembled when he covered it, but she didn't pull away. "No, ma'am. With respect, I am not."

Ms. Thornton sat back, her posture ever prim, and lifted her brows. "She does not need you." Her needling look turned onto Kenzie. "And when you find the sense to grip that truth, you know where to find me."

The woman was up and gone before he could postulate what exactly she meant. Beside him, Kenzie sighed, the edges of that long exhale jagged.

"You okay?" he asked.

"Of course."

"That was kind of...awful. Are you sure?"

"It was expected."

"You expected her to shame you like that?"

She shrugged.

"You expected her to hate me? She didn't even give me a ch—"

Kenzie lifted her face. "You have a Y chromosome. You never had a chance."

That was bizarre. But his wife left it there without another thought as she rose from the table, her hand covering the swell of her belly, as if to protect the baby.

"Kenzie?" Jackson caught the bend of her arm, and she turned to him.

"I'm okay, Jackson. She knows now. That's what was required."

"But—"

"Leave it." She held a long, serious look on him. "I need you to leave it alone, Jackson."

He couldn't make sense of it. But standing there watching her walk away, he felt certain Sean had been right.

The fear in her wasn't about him.

There wasn't much comfort in that.

Chapter Twenty-Two
(in which Jackson tells the truth)

I think it's time you brought my lovely new daughter-in-law back for a visit.

Jackson stared at the screen, rereading his mom's text. She didn't ask for much, never had. And she'd been so helpful to Kenz, calling to encourage her, posting Kenzie's creations so that they'd sell—which he was pretty sure was the reason his cabinets and fridge stayed stocked without much intervention on his part.

How could he deny Mom's kind, though innocently difficult, request? Just because things between Kenz and him were about as easy as scaling a vertical cliff didn't mean he couldn't make an effort with his mom. And Kenz liked her. Surely she'd be up for it.

Yeah. He totally knew that for sure, since Kenz kept him at what felt like the other side of the planet at all times. Especially since the night he'd held her.

He'd known that was going to work out all wrong. Knew. It.

Why? He leaned back against the truck seat and stared up at the ceiling. *Why aren't You helping here?*

Nothing.

Drenched in some kind of awful sour mood and unable to scuff it off, he left the truck and paced to the house. Kenz was home—amazingly—and was working on a design.

"Hi."

Well. A greeting even. It was his lucky day.

"Hey." The sour in him saturated his voice.

She stood, a flower in hand, and turned. Brows tucked inward, she studied him. "You okay?"

"Awesome." Whoa. He was losing it.

Her lips parted, free hand spanned the undeniable evidence of their baby. She blinked, licked her lips, and tried again. "Bad day?"

You care? With a press of his jaw, he trapped the words. "No. It's fine. Did you have plans for supper, or should I put something together for the both of us?"

Bitterness rose up further. For several days, he'd eaten every meal alone. She'd had the courtesy, at least, to text somewhere around suppertime, things like *I'm eating out.* Or *Meeting a friend, don't wait for me.* Silent jabs that said *I don't want to be with you* better than the actual words ever could.

"I'm home for the night."

Home, was it? Huh.

"Jackson, you look—"

"Mom wants us to come visit."

"Oh." She turned to lay the stem she'd been rolling between her fingers on the table. "Yes. She texted me."

"Well, that's great, Kenz. Glad you talk to someone."

"What?"

He dropped what he was sure was a glare, rubbing the back of his neck. "Nothing. So this weekend?"

"That would work for me. Do you have any jobs lined up though?"

He turned, giving her his back. What was with this sudden concern? "Nope."

He opened the fridge, searching for something for supper. "Jackson?"

Her hand warmed his lower back, the touch scalding. With a side and back step, he jolted away.

Those copper eyes grew as she stared up at him. "What's going on?"

"You tell me."

"What?"

"Don't *what* me. You know exactly what I mean. I'm not up for this game."

A furious blush flooded her pale skin, and she looked toward her bare feet. For a long stretch, it seemed she wasn't going to answer, which was apparently how she handled everything uncomfortable in her life. With silence.

"You're making me crazy, Kenz. You do know that, don't you?"

She backed up against the counter opposite him, and at the crumbling of her posture, he turned away. Watching her dissolve made him both angrier and softer, though he couldn't understand how that worked. He didn't want either.

"I'm sorry," she whispered.

"For what?" The words came out like poison.

"My mother—"

"Your mother doesn't scare me, and you know that's not what this is about."

Two beats of silence spanned the space between them.

Her voice was breathy when she started again. "That night— when we...were together."

With a look over his shoulder, he focused a glare on her. "When we made love?"

The breaking point was near. He could feel the dam within cracking. Hands shaking, pulse throbbing against his temples, he wavered in the temptation to walk away. He could go run. Or just leave. Go somewhere until the volcano inside had spewed and was done. Then they could go back to passive-aggressive, pretend-we're-fine silence.

She refused to make eye contact. "It was a mistake."

Hearing the words shouldn't have toppled him. He'd known that was what she thought. Felt.

Still.

"Why are you still here, Kenz? I'm not holding you prisoner."

"You don't want me to stay?"

"I didn't say that, and I think you know better than to think it.

I've done everything I know to show you that I want you. You keep sending it all back." Facing her again, he closed the gap between them. "You're smart. You're capable. You could figure something else out. And you know I'll take care of the baby—whatever that looks like. So why are killing me with this?"

With a stubborn lift of her chin, she masked the conflict of emotions he'd watched play on her face with anger. "I'll leave if that's what you want."

"Were you listening?"

Her jaw trembled, and she looked away.

"Man!" She was so stubborn. She had but to take one step. One freaking step, and he'd pull her in close. One little hint that she'd try with him, and he'd be ready to do it all again. He must be insane.

He gripped the counter beside her, arms twitching. "I can't do this." Leaning back, he looked up again, aching for some kind of relief from heaven. *Something?*

Nothing. He looked back down at her. "It's like you have me, Kenz, but I can't have you."

Her shoulders trembled, and she laid her palms over the swell of their baby.

"I'm just a man. How do you expect me to live like that?"

"I don't know," she whispered. With one hand, she pushed the weight of her loose waves off her face. Those long, slender fingers shook.

The force of the storm within calmed, and the winds of fury settled into swirls of ache. Did he want her to leave?

No.

This is too hard!

As quietness gelled thick between them and the remnants of what had just blown up settled into a mess in his heart, a sense of direction gripped firm. Once again, heaven spoke, and this time, the words embedded.

Let her have you.

A simple directive. But it felt impossible. He had. He'd let her have him.

No conditions.

Could he live like that? This...this was beyond him. What if he said no?

The answer was silence. Devastating silence.

Kenz sniffed, pulling him out of inside himself, drawing his attention back to her. A scared, lonely woman who had no idea what love was. A beautiful, broken woman who needed desperately to know.

He still felt incapable.

Help.

Something firm and stable gripped his mind, his heart.

"All right," he whispered.

Kenz startled, turned her wet face up to him. Tender pain flowed into the places that had only been hard and angry moments ago.

"All right, Kenz." He lifted one hand, fingers still trembling, and cupped the side of her face.

Her lips parted, a near-silent *what* lifting on her exhale as she searched his eyes.

Swallowing, he forced himself to unshutter the emotion that felt so raw and vulnerable. Full exposure. He felt his heart empty before her.

"You have me."

***

Helen didn't waste a moment pretending casual interest. The second Mackenzie waddled through the Murphy's front door, Jackson's mom had her engulfed.

"Look at this!" She stepped back from the full hug, a hand falling to rest on Mackenzie's baby bump. "So beautiful." Their eyes met, and Helen smiled with love on high beam. "I do believe pregnancy becomes you, Kenz. I'm so glad you could talk my son into a visit so I wouldn't miss all of it."

Once again, Mackenzie hardly knew what to say. She didn't think being round and awkward was becoming, and she certainly hadn't talked Jackson into anything. She'd barely talked to him at all in the five days since Helen had texted, asking them to come visit. Hadn't known what to say to her husband. *What do you say to a man who tells you You have me with his whole hurting heart sheened in his intense gaze? How do you tell him not to give you that kind of power when you're certain that, with all you don't know about relationships, you'll wreck him with it?*

Nothing. That was what she'd gone with. She hadn't said anything. Just like she didn't know what to say to Helen.

"Come on now, Mom." With one hand solid on Mackenzie's lower back, Jackson leaned to hug his mom, the move warm and inclusive. And awkward. "You know I wanted to come."

Helen smirked. "Two visits in six months. I am moving up in the world."

Jackson loved his mother—his family. Mackenzie heard it in the way he spoke with them on the phone, about them to her. Perhaps Helen didn't know the gem she had in her son. Perhaps Mackenzie didn't know what she had right in front of her either.

Why did he love so stubborn like that? What was in it for him?

***

Jackson followed his dad down the stairs. The basement. Again? He hadn't volunteered this time, and two nights on the hide-a-bed didn't seem like a thoughtful arrangement for his pregnant wife.

What was Mom thinking?

"We thought you'd be better set up down there," she'd said. "Since you claimed it the last time."

"Are you expecting someone for the room upstairs?" Jackson asked.

"Jacob and Kate said they'd come sometime tomorrow."

Nice. Failed to mention that in the *I miss you. Bring your wife back to see me* text. When had Mom become such a sneak?

He capped the rising irritation as he carried Kenzie's bag and jostled his own, slung over his shoulder. It might be better this way anyway. The basement was more private. He could endure his wife's attempt at keeping a polar distance between them in the noninvasive solitude. Plus, they'd survived the pull-out before...

Three feet behind Dad, he rounded the stairwell and walked into the family-room-turned-guest room.

Jackson stopped cold, and Kenz nearly collided with his back. Whoa.

"What is this?" he asked.

Mom made a little squeal behind him. "Surprise!" She clapped her hands as she slipped around Jackson and Mackenzie to sidle up beside Dad. Smile on full blast, she actually bounced. "What do you think?"

Mouth hinged open, he took in the queen-size sleigh bed covered in a soft cream comforter. The dark wood gleamed, setting off the lighter bedding. On either side was a matching nightstand, and a complimenting highboy dresser posted up against the far wall.

"Wow, it's really nice, Mom."

"Yeah?" Still smiling, Mom bit her bottom lip and looked at Kenzie. "Do you like it, honey?"

"It's beautiful." Kenz stepped forward until she could touch the shiny fabric of the bedding.

"The duvet could change, if it's not your taste. That's an easy fix. But also, if the style of the furniture isn't your taste, we can get something else. I just wanted to have something here to surprise you with."

"It's your house, Mom. Not sure why you would change it on our account."

Dad chuckled. "He didn't get it, Helen. I told you they would be confused."

Puzzled, Jackson shifted his look from parent to parent. Mom's smile inched higher.

"It's not ours. It's yours. Our wedding gift to you, though it's terribly late."

Kenzie's hand fell to her side. "What?" The word came out breathy.

Mom's smile softened. "Your wedding gift. And—" She walked toward the highboy, her aim for a large table covered by one of her floral tablecloths. First a wink and then she flipped the cloth back with the flick of one hand. "Your baby gift."

Not a table. A crib.

Still at the bed, Kenz sucked in a breath. Jackson's heart squeezed. How could something be so kind and so painful in a single moment?

As if magnetically drawn, Kenz stepped toward the dark wooden crib. Her hand slid forward, and with a look of shock, she caressed the smooth top rail.

"It converts to a toddler bed when you're ready." Mom cupped the bend of Kenzie's elbow. Several still breaths passed, and then, sounding a bit unsure, she said, "Do you like it?"

Kenz continued to gaze at the gift. "It's beautiful."

She liked it. More than liked it—the look on his wife's face was pure wonder. Almost as much as it had been the day they'd glimpsed their unborn baby. The squeeze of everything hard between them eased as gratitude washed in its place. Whatever complications were between him and Kenz, this was a beautiful, loving gesture on the part of his parents, and it had affected his wife in a way that was rare.

Why does she shield away this side of herself? As much as she did the fiery version of herself, Kenz kept this soft, wonderstruck version of the woman she was closely tied within, leaving only a mask of indifference more often than anything else. Was this a natural tendency or something learned?

The harsh green stare of Colleen Thornton washed through his mind. Learned. It had been taught.

"Jackson?"

He startled to find his mother's attention on him. Fixing a quick—but genuine—smile, he strode toward her. "It's amazing, Mom. Dad. Thank you." After a lingering hug for his mom, he turned to his dad.

"Your mom was so excited about this." Dad clapped his back. "Don't worry though—I'll bring a couple of the boys down with me and we'll deliver and set up at your house whenever you're ready." Dad moved to side hug Kenzie. "And we have a suite picked out for this room too, so you'll never have to spend another uncomfortable night on the pull-out again."

Though she looked uncertain under Dad's attention, Kenzie's

expression remained soft. Mom gripped her hand while Dad kept an arm anchored on her shoulders.

"This is so delayed," Mom said. "We hoped you didn't think we weren't excited about your marriage."

"No." Voice still wispy, Kenzie looked surprised.

Truth be told, Jackson had wondered. But only a little, and likely because of the guilt he battled for lying to his parents.

The lightness of the moment sank. He was still lying to his parents. Still involving Kenzie in that lie. And the bigger truth was, the future didn't look any more certain than it had at Christmas.

***

"Hey, Dad."

Jackson walked into the workshop off the garage, his steps heavy and slow. He didn't have any idea where to start. Didn't want to have this conversation.

"Hi, Jack. Come out to help me with the material?" Dad was double-checking the order he'd picked up from the lumber yard down the mountain. Come Monday he'd be on site for a new project, and Dad had a thing about double-checking his material so he wasn't caught *in my boxers on a snowy day*—his words—at the beginning of a build.

"Sure. Got a list?" Jackson held out a hand, and Dad grabbed a clipboard from the bench to pass to him.

For a time, they worked in silence. Jackson counted two-by-four studs while Dad worked on hardware inventory. The familiar routine eased a bit of the edginess pricking at Jackson. He'd done this since he was five, working at his dad's side. Had made the transition into contracting in electrical work fairly smooth, and he'd carried the same habit of preparedness with him from Dad's side to Sean's.

"Your mom was sure thrilled you could come this weekend." Dad broke the silence.

"I'm glad it worked. Didn't have a gig."

"That's unusual for you now, it sounds like."

Jackson lifted a brow and glanced at him.

Dad grinned. "Kenz. She tells your mother that you work the clubs most weekends. Thursdays too. Seems they text a lot. Your mom is delighted about that."

After a light chuckle, Jackson nodded. "I'm grateful to Mom for that. Means more than you know that she's so good to Kenz."

"Did you expect otherwise?"

He shrugged. Hadn't known what to expect, if he was going to be honest. But that begged the rest of the story...

Which was why he'd come out there. Might as well begin there.

"The thing is..." A long breath. A settled look on his dad.

He was listening.

Man, why was this so hard?

"Son?"

"I didn't tell you everything. About Kenz and me." It was hot in there. So hot.

"You're..." Dad straddled a stool at his workbench. "You're married, right?"

So close to the real issue. Dad had always been quick with the subtexts.

"Yes. We're married. We got married in Vegas, just like I said. But the thing is..." He drew in another deep breath. "We'd never met before."

Dad's brows pushed inward. "Never met?"

"Not once. We met at a club that Friday night. I was sulking about the marathon, because I didn't make the time I needed for Boston. The guy I was with suggested bourbon, and I was in the mood to comply. Somewhere in the early part of the night, a beautiful ginger walked in. Serious, copper eyes. Lovely round face adorably sprayed with freckles. She had a look—the kind that said she was looking for something—and I decided to go see what it was."

"Mackenzie."

Jackson nodded. "She was frustrated with work, felt defeated because her MCAT wasn't what she needed it to be for medical school, and tired of hearing about what needed to be done next from her mother." Jackson stopped as the intact pieces of that

night replayed. If he could go back...

Indeed, if he could. And yet, as his mind replayed the image of her across the room, her face a mix of vulnerability and defeat, he was certain he would have still sought her out. The moment her eyes connected with his, he'd been caught. Reeled in by something powerful and unnamed. He'd needed to know her name. Wanted to know what would make those full lips smile...

"How does that get you married, Jackson?"

"We...drank. A lot."

Dad's brows lifted, his mouth flat.

Shame burned through his veins, and Jackson could no longer keep his focus on the man across from him. Instead, he studied the floor, wondering how much smaller a man could feel. He reached for the phone in his back pocket, opened the file he'd told himself at least a hundred times to delete, and slid the screen to his father.

Forced to hear it all over again. He squeezed his eyes shut while the slurred vows, the inebriated giggles, and the careless shout *Meet my wife!* replayed from the video. With a hand at his forehead, he rubbed his eyebrows, waiting for his father's outrage.

The video ended. Silence reigned.

When Jackson finally gathered the courage to look up, he found his vision blurred.

"You're still married." Dad's voice came low, gravelly.

He nodded. "Yes."

"Because of the baby?"

Throat tight, he could only nod.

Dad passed the phone back to him, his expression disappointment and concern. After several tense moments, he sat back down. "I would have sworn I saw more between you two."

"I love her." The words barely passed his lips.

"And Kenz?"

He shook his head. No, his wife did not love him, and the confession pressed on him was like a blade across his heart.

"But she needs you."

"I ruined her life." With both hands, he raked his fingers

through his hair. "Now, I don't know what to do."

Cocooned in misery, he didn't hear his father rise, nor the steps he made to close the space between them. The feel of his father's work-hardened arms around him came as a shock, breaking him.

"Ah, son." Only two words. Not of anger. Not of condemnation.

Jackson wept like a child in his father's arms.

Chapter Twenty-Three

(in which Mackenzie makes a decision)

Saturday seeped by like a gentle river. In no hurry to go, and yet the steady current slipped on. Helen and Mackenzie spent the morning in the greenhouse and then out in the garden. Together they explored possibilities for late-summer designs. Farmhouse chic and yet clean and simple. Mackenzie found herself introduced to the humble yet versatile possibilities of zinnias, sunflowers of surprising varieties, sedum, and ornamental grasses. Together they explored new combinations, and by two in the afternoon, they had six new arrangements photographed.

During lunch break, Jacob and Kate made an entrance. Helen made her rounds of exuberant hugs—and part of Mackenzie wondered if the woman wasn't dressing up her smile a little bit. After spending the morning with her mother-in-law, it seemed that her easy joy had shifted a bit toward the forced kind. On the heels of that thought, Jacob turned to Mackenzie, eyebrow raised, and then pinned an unsmiling look on Jackson.

"Still married, huh?"

Jackson drew up, and for a heartbeat, Mackenzie saw fire burn in his look. Just as quickly, though, he grinned, moved in for a brotherly hug, and smacked Jacob's back.

"Keep working on that humor, buddy. You'll get it."

Jackson's dad chuckled, and his mom shifted the attention to

the food spread on the table. Feathers smoothed. Subtle insults pushed to an undercurrent.

After lunch, the conversation between Helen and Mackenzie turned to Jackson. It was as if Helen could read Mackenzie's questions about how Jackson had handled his brother.

"Of my boys," Helen had said, "I think Jackson is the fullest of contradictions."

An irresistible opening if ever there was one.

"What do you mean by that?"

Helen laughed. "He is both serious and full of humor. Light and dark. He feels deeply but keeps most things superficial. Don't you think?"

Yes. Mackenzie did think. And the unexpected depth of the man was what drew her and also frightened her. She could fall into the deep, be swallowed by it. Then what?

"Flawed man that he is, he does love well though, doesn't he?"

Suddenly Mackenzie felt caught. How to answer? If she was honest, she would say yes. Jackson loved very well. Too well, and it was unnerving. His stubborn affection pried at her defenses, disrupting her plans. Foiling her attempts to maintain distance.

"Kenz?" Helen stopped her floral designing and pressed both palms on the counter. "Is my son good to you?"

"He is." The answer was rushed. True, but forced.

"Is there a lie in that?"

"None at all."

"Then what has you hiding?"

Direct. She shouldn't be surprised to find that the woman who raised Jackson was also direct.

"He is...surprising." Careful there, or she could come too near the truth.

"Surprising?" Helen began cleaning the mess they'd made.

She couldn't betray him. Didn't want to betray herself. With a slow alignment of words, Mackenzie said, "I don't understand where his depth comes from. It...confuses me sometimes."

Helen stopped clearing the stems from the counter and reached to cup her cheek with the other. "Jackson knows the wounds of

rejection. Because of the cleft lip, and the long struggle with being different, he is sensitive. But he also refuses to let people defeat him, and sometimes he uses his humor as armor—or worse, as a weapon. Not always—he had several lessons growing up about how far is too far and when to quit. Through it all, he discovered a strength as a boy that it seems few young men ever find."

Once again, an irresistible setup. "What was that?"

"He is loved. Deeply loved by the God who does not look upon his face searching for mistakes but looks upon the man as one He died for."

The memory of her first morning in Jackson's home ran through her mind, the morning he told her why he went to church.

It was about Jesus. About being loved and redeemed. At the time, she'd been touched by his sincerity of the moment, but doubted it really mattered in real life. After all, she was pregnant because of him. Well, partly because of him.

But the past six months had shown her otherwise. What Jackson believed played out in his life in a way that left her very little room to ignore what was right in front of her.

Mackenzie found herself in desperate need of time to think. And with a longing for the kind of love that drove her husband.

***

"Know where my wife went?" Jackson spoke to his mom's back as she uploaded images to her blog.

Mom glanced over her shoulder. "She said she needed a walk in the fresh mountain air."

"Alone?"

A chuckle shook her shoulders. "She's pregnant, Jackson. Not an invalid."

Huh. Apparently, his affinity for Kenzie's underlying feistiness came from home. "Know where she went?"

"The bluff, I think." Mom spun in her chair, catching Jackson before he turned to go. "Jackson, I wanted to say something to you."

Oh no. That was never a good intro. "Okay..."

"Jacob and Kate..."

Shaking his head, he held up a hand. "Mom, please. Can we all just let this go already?"

Sighing, Mom looked at him with a gentle smile. "I know. I'm sorry I've been kind of ridiculous over it. Sometimes I still see my little boy who got picked on way too much, and I get all mama bear. I didn't like what she did to you. Wasn't very happy with your brother about it either."

"Yeah. I know. Here's the thing, Mom. I'm really fine. Have been, even before Kenz."

"I realize that. But there's something maybe you don't realize. Jacob and Kate, they're not always fine. When you start off a relationship with lies and manipulation, well, you've got a foundation of lies and manipulation. And lately they've been struggling with some other issues on top of an already shaky foundation. Makes a tenuous marriage even more difficult. I don't know what happened between you and your brother before they got here today—I know Jacob gives out way more than he gets. But, well, I was just talking with Kenzie about how you love well. You do, and I'm proud of you for it. Your brother—he needs it. He'll never tell you why, but he needs that love too."

A *be nice to Jacob* chat tacked on to a compliment about loving well, he most definitely didn't deserve. Following his emotional confession to his dad, that just made the day even better. Jackson gripped his neck, fought against the tension in his shoulders.

"Jackson—"

"I got it, Mom."

She stood and slipped an arm around his waist. "I am proud of you, son."

Great. Add guilt to everything else. She had no idea. Certainly, she would—he knew better than to think that Dad would keep a secret like this from Mom. They didn't roll like that. By this time tomorrow, she'd be rescinding all of those nice things she'd just said. He rubbed a hand over the stubble on his face, his index finger catching the bump of his scar.

Dad had offered the hope of God's healing and redemption

She rolled her bottom lip under her teeth, and when she blinked, a tear slipped onto her cheek. "I don't know."

Confusion eased from his expression, though concern still pulled on his brow. His touch fell away, and Mackenzie fought the urge to fold herself against him.

What if he could be her shelter? The dream she'd never been allowed to have? And what if she was his? Instead of him ruining her life—and her destroying him—they could make a beautiful life together?

Such a tantalizing possibility. But some of her questions would remain forever unanswered. More, she might never know who she truly was. What she really wanted.

"Did I tell you that my grandparents live in San Diego?" She sniffed, sat straighter. She was certain she had, at some point when he'd asked about her family.

He watched her, an intensity in his stare, and nodded.

"I think I should go."

The pulse that throbbed through his neck leapt. He turned to face the view, leaning his elbows against his knees as his shoulders rounded. "For how long?"

"I don't know," she whispered.

His silence ached as he stared toward the mountains. She was killing him. Acutely, she felt the pain pierce her own heart. But it was necessary.

The beauty of the view faded until she only knew him, broken by her side. This moment would forever be burned in with agony. Even if she knew how to make him understand, she doubted it would help.

"Jackson." Her voice broke on his name.

He lifted his folded hands, pressed them against his forehead, and then nodded. "All right."

"All right?"

"I told you that you are free to do what you want." The look he turned on her was all pain and love, both open for her to see in full. "I meant it."

A tear slipped onto her cheek. With a tender touch, he traced its path with the pad of his thumb. When he leaned down, she lifted her chin. Met his mouth while another tear slipped from the corner of her eye.

The kiss was slow and gentle, as if he was savoring each touch, each breath. Because he knew it might be the last.

He pulled back enough to meet her gaze.

"You can always come home, Kenz." The moisture that sheened his dark eyes overflowed into a trickle that followed the curve of his nose. He caught her lips with one final brush of his and then removed his touch entirely.

"Always." The word was rough on his voice. And then he was gone.

Chapter Twenty-Four
(in which Mackenzie asks about love)

It took a while to identify what felt so strange—besides not seeing Jackson every day and missing him so much. While that was unexpected, it wasn't what felt like squeezing into her pre-pregnancy jeans and pretending they fit perfect.

It was the isolation.

Alone in the large, richly finished sunroom at her grandmother's in San Diego, understanding snapped like a floodlight. This isolation had been her life's standard for virtually all her years, until Jackson. She'd lived in a tiny kingdom of her mother's making. A small universe in which all outsiders were either a threat or a liability.

She'd never realized it. Not once. Not when she was lonely as a child and then as a young woman. Not when she found making friends and interacting at college a challenge she'd not been equipped to meet.

Only just now, with a cup of orange juice—not a smoothie—in her right hand, gazing at a view of the Pacific that by all accounts was stunning, and feeling only alone. A tremble raced through her, and the juice sloshed, making tiny waves within its confined little ocean.

A hand to the babe that grew within, she shut her eyes, pushing at the great emptiness of it. Behind her lids, she saw the words

Jackson penned, now safely kept in the bottom of her drawer after she'd discovered them tucked within an envelope and waiting for her on the seat in her car.

Mackenzie. I'll never get this out, but I need to. So I'm writing it.

I am ashamed that I can't remember much of the vows I gave you the day we married. I am ashamed of pretty much every part of that day.

But never of you. Don't ever think that I'm ashamed to call you my wife. I am not. In fact, there is a great, growing part of me that is thankful for the reckless mess of that day. From it came you. From it came this son or daughter of ours, a child I already deeply love.

I want to remember the vows I give you. I want to give them on purpose. With a sober mind, a sure heart, and a promise to you that I mean them. Because I do.

So,

I, Jackson Murphy, take you, Mackenzie Thornton, to be my wife.

I promise to hold you safely in the shelter of my heart.

I promise to love you, to honor you, and to keep you above all others. No matter where you are. What you choose to do. I will love you.

From this day forward, in sickness and health, for better or worse, richer or poorer, I give you my vow.

You have me. You will always have me.

Until death.

Tears lined the rim of her eyes. *Jackson. What have you done?*

He'd removed the blinders she'd been comfortable with. Invaded lies that she'd long accepted as truth. More than anything though, he'd shown her something she'd always thought was an illusion.

Love.

Deep, unselfish, stubborn love.

How could she have found that in a man she'd married while drunk in Sin City? The spectrum between what had happened—and what she'd assumed about him—and what was becoming clear about who he really was simply astonished her.

Eyes still closed, she let the memory of his goodbye linger in

the moment. Her loaded car—thanks to him—sat out front.
He'd made her an orange smoothie—just as he had nearly every
single day since she'd moved in. Standing in the kitchen, ready to
go to work, as if this was a morning just like any other, his hand
gently traveled the curve of her face. Clear agony in his eyes, he'd
whispered his goodbye.

"I don't want to be the man who wrecked your life, Kenz. If
that means letting you go, then..." He'd blinked. Rolled his lips
together. Then sniffed. "Bye, beautiful." He kissed her as he had
before, gently near the temple, whispered "I love you," then
disappeared out the door.

She was leaving him. Though unspoken, they both understood
what was happening. How could he love like that?

His mother's words seeped through that tender memory, the
ones about Jackson loving well. Because he knew he was loved by
God.

That seemed like such a great mystery—especially to a girl
who'd grown up thinking that God was a myth of Disney
proportions—and one that was not to be tolerated any more than
Walt's imaginative retellings. And yet, standing in her
grandparent's home, watching the amber glow of the lowering
sun made brilliant by the rolling waters of the ocean, that
mystery settled in a place within. A place that was deep and
foreign.

The empty place.

Are You real? And if You are, do You really love like that?

She had no idea where to find the answers. Still, an answer
seemed to fill that empty spot.

I AM.

A truth unknown and yet revealed. Somehow. Another
mystery. But undeniable.

Can You love me like that?

The emptiness continued to diminish. Something warm and
sweet and so very big that the ocean beyond the floor-to-ceiling
window seemed but a drop. More mystery. She surrendered to it,
and as she did, a highlight reel of her life since she'd married

Jackson touched her mind. As those moments of Jackson's tenderness soaked into her heart, that bigger *something* seemed to make Jackson's love glow with a glory that was beyond. As if it were not just his.

It was platinum, otherworldly, and breathtakingly beautiful.

What if...

Jackson's words, whispered desperately as they'd stood in her entry after Christmas. He'd meant what if they could make their massive mistake of a marriage work. But as the memory turned, the whisper changed. The voice became inaudible, but so very real. The question turned and dived deeper.

What if you knew, Mackenzie? What if you saw what love could be, and you would begin to see the Source behind it?

What if you knew I've been waiting to tell you...

What? Her heart stalled as she waited to *feel* what it was *He* wanted to tell her. The world paused around her. As if everything in her life hinged on this moment. It seemed there were hosts in heaven leaning in, waiting to hear what *He* would say. Waiting along with her, breath caught, hearts gripped.

"What?" she whispered.

You have Me.

Her jaw trembled as the barrier around her heart shattered.

***

Does the God who loves Jackson love me too?

She stared at the text. Heat smeared her face as she thought of how impulsively she'd sent it to Helen. Wondered if Helen would think she was nuts. Worried that her mother-in-law (should she still think of Jackson's mom that way?) would be upset to find out that Mackenzie didn't believe like Jackson did.

But for all the reasons she had to not ask, she had to know.

No, she already knew.

Didn't she?

The throb of her heart ached as she stared at the phone screen. She could have asked Jackson. Maybe should have, to keep all this between them. But she couldn't. She'd already carved enough pain into his heart. The thought of making him hurt more was unbearable.

As the agony in his eyes passed through her memory once again, she turned her attention from the phone in her hand to the letter lying on her bed, unfolded and spread with his handwriting facing up.

You have me. You will always have me.

She'd left him. He hadn't begged her not to. But this promise?

No doubt stirred within her about his sincerity. He meant it, whether she went home to him or not. Jackson would love her for the rest of his life. Because he promised to.

That was flat out amazing.

The phone in her hand vibrated, and she had to blink away the blur of threatening tears to read the incoming text.

He loves you. So much, my daughter.

Whether Helen intended it or not, Mackenzie read a double meaning in the answer.

If she were back in Vegas and placing a wager, she'd bet that it was indeed intended.

And she would have won.

***

Jackson stared at the room. The beautiful sleigh bed—Kenz had called it beautiful, so he thought of it that way. The perfect cream bedding—his wife had told Mom it was perfect. So it was. The rich dark wood of the matching dresser.

The force of Dad's hand squeezed his shoulder. "Your mom called me. She's heard from Kenz."

Surprise snapped his head up, and he turned enough to meet his father's look.

"She asked if God loves her."

Jackson's eyes closed, moisture lining the seams. "I've really made a mess of everything."

Dad chuckled low. "That seems to be what we do in this life. Good thing we have a redeeming God."

Though he forced his eyes open again, he couldn't look into Dad's face. Instead, he found the wall in his sights as he nodded.

"He still loves you, Jack. And He is always in the redeeming business."

Another nod. He knew that was true. Knew that God could...

"More, your wife wants to know if your God loves her too."

Dad paused on that, his silence adding weight to the statement.

Please let her know that You do.

"We're praying for you both, Jack." Dad's hand on his shoulder squeezed again. "And for the record, your mom and I, we love you both. That's not going to change."

Dad moved away, took himself out of the house. Probably went straight to the truck, where Connor would be waiting after having helped move the new furniture into Jackson's room, and his old bedroom set to the basement—which was where Jackson would be sleeping from here on out. This room, this furniture, was for his wife. He'd keep it that way.

Emotion shook through him as he thought about the crib in the room down the hall. The room that still smelled of warm orange blossoms and clean mint—of Mackenzie Thornton Murphy, who might never go by that name again.

The painting of his life seemed a smeared disaster.

Jackson rolled his shoulders against the wall and sank to the floor.

I keep hoping for a Bob Ross thing. I know You can, God. Now I'm trying to accept that maybe it's just not Your plan.

He had no idea how to live with that.

found their way beside her nose. "No. Start here." She pointed to a line on the page.

Blinking, he cleared his throat. "I want to remember the vows I give you. I want to give them on purpose. With a sober mind, a sure heart, and a promise to you that I mean them. Because I do. So..." He drew another quivering breath and moved his gaze to find hers again. The place in his chest that had felt crushed and abandoned began to expand. "I, Jackson Murphy, take you, Mackenzie Thornton, to be my wife. I promise to hold you safely in the shelter of my heart. I promise to love you, to honor you, and to keep you above all others. No matter where you are. What you choose to do. I will love you.

"From this day forward, in sickness and health, for better or worse, richer or poorer, I give you my vow. You have me. You will always have me. Until death."

As a fresh tear slipped near her nose, he cradled her face, tracing the trail of her tears as one of his own leaked from the corner of his eye.

She covered his wrists with her hands. "Jackson, I don't remember the vows we spoke either, and honestly, I doubt that I meant them. I thought marriage would smother me. Turns out, with you, I finally see who I really am, and I am truly free to be that woman. I didn't know what love is. I wouldn't now, except there you are. Loving me in spite of myself. You love well, and I want to also. I want to spend a lifetime of loving well with you. So..." She inhaled and stepped closer, and as his heart nearly exploded with awe and joy, she unfolded a slip of paper she'd held tucked into her palm. She breathed a nervous, teary laugh. "I've never been to a—I mean except..."

She pressed her lips together and shook her head. "I had to Google this. So here it goes. I, Mackenzie Thornton, take you, Jackson Murphy, to be my husband. Before God, and with a sober mind and a heart that is sure, I promise I will not abandon you. I will choose love, even when it is hard. I will choose forgiveness, even when there is anger. I will choose honor, even when it might cost me."

Silent cries overcame her. She closed her eyes, lifted her face to his, and then opened them. There were several blinks until the tears cleared. "You have me, Jackson." Her whispered voice quivered. "You will always have me. Until death."

Breath stolen as if he'd just finished that run two minutes before, and not ten, Jackson leaned down until their foreheads met. He breathed her in, savoring the smell of oranges and warm sunshine, and his heart surged. "Are you sure?"

With a small push up, she moved to take his mouth with her lips. After a nip that was not nearly enough, she whispered, "I love you, Jackson. I want to be your wife."

Overwhelming amazement and joy made him dizzy. He'd never experienced a miracle quite like that. Hands sliding from her neck, over her shoulders, then around her back, he pulled her in to kiss her more fully, but as his mouth moved against hers, the sound of clapping jarred him from the dimension that was theirs alone.

"I now pronounce you husband and wife!" Sean beamed from the walking path to the left, his phone poised in camera position, and then gave a two-finger whistle. Several other early morning walkers and joggers had stopped to witness their vows and were now cheering.

Though heat brushed his cheeks, Jackson met Kenzie's forehead with his own again, his arms around her. The swell of life in her belly pressed between them, and the punch of a leg made itself known. He laughed as he moved to place a palm over their little soccer player.

Kenzie chuckled too, lowering a hand to cover his. "Can he do that?"

"Who?"

"Sean. Can he—"

"Legally? I doubt it." Jackson smiled. Winked. "Good thing we're already married, huh?"

The grin that lifted her lovely, so very kissable mouth glowed. "Yes. It's a very good thing."

"Kiss the bride!" Someone shouted.

He didn't mind if he did. Apparently, neither did she.

Epilogue

"Two hours, fifty-two minutes, twenty-eight seconds. About." Mackenzie beamed at the man bent over at the side of the Strip, hands on his knees, dripping sweat and panting. Neon lights gleamed off his wet body and made his drenched hair appear as various shades of electric green, blue, and orange.

"About, huh?" With a grin that did delightfully crazy things to her insides, he looked at her. "Didn't you use the watch?"

"You have one of your own, right?"

He stood, draped a disgustingly wet arm over her, and pressed an equally gooey kiss against her forehead. "There's that bit of fire I love."

Ducking out of his slippery arm, she smiled. "Just for you."

Jackson laughed, taking her hand. "Is this acceptable?"

"You are literally oozing sweat from every pore."

"I just ran a marathon."

"You did." She squeezed his hand and looked up at him. He'd done it, and she was so proud. "You qualified for Boston."

His grin leapt into a full-blown smile. "That's true."

"So?"

"We'll see."

"We'll see? This time last year, that was everything to you."

That champion smile tempered as love softened the teasing in his eyes. "Things change."

She glanced over the crowd that milled around the finish line, looking for the faces that were certain to be lit with excitement. There. Jackson's parents stood side by side, and yes, they were glowing. As was Connor, except the glowing part. He did grin though. The other boys were around somewhere, because everyone wanted to witness the *public vows* she and Jackson would exchange later that night to celebrate their first anniversary.

And there, in Helen's arms, little Bobbie Joy Murphy drooled and waved her pudgy baby hands, the fuzz of her red hair sticking straight up in the dry, static air.

"Yes," Mackenzie breathed as her heart nearly burst with joy. "Things do change."

Like everything. Her entire worldview had shifted. All because of an insanely stupid mistake that had happened right there in Vegas one year before. A mistake that, as Jackson said, God had so perfectly Bob Rossed.

Jackson stopped weaving through the crowd, pulling her to a halt beside him. "Thank God things change."

She leaned, kissing her disgustingly sweaty husband with perfect joy.

Thank God indeed.

the end.

Dear reader

I hope you enjoyed Jackson and Mackenzie's story and that it encouraged you to love like God loves. I'd so appreciate it if you'd leave your thoughts on the story in the form of a review on Amazon or Goodreads (or both!). You'll find further inspiration and encouragement on The Potter's House Books Website (www.pottershousebooks.com) and by reading the other books in the series. Read them all and be encouraged and uplifted!

Jennifer Rodewald

Find all the books on Amazon and on The Potter's House Books website:

Book 1: *The Hope We Share*, by Juliette Duncan

Book 2: *Beyond the Deep*, by Kristen M. Fraser

Book 3: *Honor's Reward*, by Mary Manners

Book 4: *Hands of Grace*, by Brenda S. Anderson

Book 5: *Always You*, by Jen Rodewald

Book 6: *Her Cowboy Forever*, by Dora Hiers

Book 7: *Changed Somehow*, by Chloe Flanagan

Books 8: *Fragrance of Forgiveness*, by Delia Latham

Books 9: *When Love Abounds* by Juliette Duncan

Book 10: *More Than This* by Kristen M. Fraser

Book 11: *Faith's Favor* by Mary Manners

Book 12: *Song of Mercy* by Brenda S. Anderson

Book 13: *In Spite of Ourselves* by Jennifer Rodewald

And more to come...

Also, In Spite of Ourselves is the second book in Jennifer Rodewald's Murphy Brothers Stories! Book one, if you missed it, is Always You, and you can find it on Amazon! Book three, Everything Behind Us, will be released on January 12, 2021. If you want more details, or to know when the preorder is live, please join my newsletter by visiting me at **authorjenrodewald.com** (pssttt... there's a free book involved!)

About the Author

 Jennifer Rodewald, a.k.a. J. Rodes, lives on the wide plains somewhere near the middle of Nowhere. A coffee addict and storyteller, she also wears the hats of mom, teacher, and friend. Mostly, she loves Jesus and wants to see others fall in love with Him too.

She would love to hear from you! Please visit her at https://authorjenrodewald.com/ or at www.facebook.com/authorjenrodewald.

Made in the USA
Middletown, DE
11 November 2021